Not Forgotten
a novel

EMMA DONALDSON

ISBN-13: 978-0615577500
ISBN-10: 0615577504

Cover photograph by Deane Erts

For Eleanor, Katherine & Mary.
You are not forgotten.

MEMORY

When the rain swept across the roof and the thunder cracked, demanding respect like Father's voice when he was mad, Little Andrew would roll over in bed until he felt his big sister's warm body. He waited like that until she wrapped him in a protective embrace and silently stroked his hair with his head cradled under her chin, then, he knew she was awake.

"Tell me about when we grow up," he asked Laura, hoping for a story to transport him to the grown up world, letting him forget the storm surrounding the house.

"Little boys who don't get their sleep don't have time to grow up," she half heartedly scolded.

"Tell me about you," he asked, knowing she had a weakness for dreaming about what her own grown up life would be. "Tell me what happens to you when you become as beautiful as Grandmother Julia when she was young."

They both giggled. Grandmother Julia was so old neither could envision what she must have looked like when she was young. It was her own words she used to inform everyone of the beauty she had once possessed.

"Do you think I'll ever be that pretty?" she teased.

"Oh, yes, Laura. Prettier," he turned around and faced her in the darkness.

"You, my handsome brother, will have to make sure only the kindest man will be allowed to marry me then."

"What else?"

"I'll get married and have lots of girls and boys. I'll be the best mother to them."

"Like Mother?" He asked. She did not answer right away so he concentrated on watching Laura's face in the flashes of the lightning that lit the room with whiteness, unlike the yellow glow from the kerosene lamp. In those intense glimpses he saw of his sister, the lightning flashes seemed to magnify a raw emotion in her he could feel in the pit of his stomach. Little Andrew could sense that Mother did not love Laura like she loved him. He did not know why. Mother was so good to him.

"Like Mother, I suppose," she reluctantly agreed.

His mother's face he could see clearly in his imagination. The scar across the bridge of her nose reminded him of Grandmother Julia's doll. Grandmother Julia loved that doll. Words could not describe the tender look that came across her face when she gazed upon the doll, despite the cracks filled with yellowed glue marring the doll's forehead. If Grandmother Julia could love this imperfect doll, it seemed incongruous that she could not love her own daughter with the scar across the front of her face. Maybe that was why Mother didn't love Laura as much as he and Harry. Maybe that was the ways of mothers and daughters.

"It will be fun to have your children to play with, Laura," he tried to cheer her with a distraction.

"Silly boy, you'll be their uncle. You will be all grown up. You won't play with them, you'll be an adult."

Seeing his sister's sadness she did not have time to hide, scared him as he realized that he and Laura and Harry and Mother and Father were individuals, and being a family would not be strong enough nor reason enough for them to always be together, fanning out around his world and life. Being alone and without them was frightening to think about.

"I don't want to grow up."

"Why would you say that?"

"I don't want to die."

"Oh, Andrew, you are going to live to be an old man, I can see you with wrinkles and white hair."

"But I'm afraid to die. I'd be all alone. What if you and Mother and Father and Harry forget me?"

"You won't be alone. I promise we won't forget you."

Little Andrew lay silently, trying to listen to what the rain would bring. Father would not worry about the dry crops and Mother would have water to wash the laundry and the chickens would have grass to eat again. The rain would fill the dry creek beds and give Little Andrew something to play in, where he could pretend to fish. He wished the rain could fill him up and give him relief from the new fears he had just discovered.

CHAPTER 1

Laura lay in her bed and could feel her body dying. It was a slow decent into a weakened state that would end with obituary notices printed in newspapers in towns where no one was likely to remember her. Outside the window, hanging from a black metal Sheppard's hook, sitting crooked in the ground, an empty bird feeder swayed in the breeze. The last winter winds blew against the north side of the building. From the angle of her bed, Laura could not see the hopeful chickadees that flew away when they found nothing nor could she see the people she heard coming and going out the door. The sheet that lay between her and the vinyl bed cushion gave little comfort to her flesh which sometimes felt like her bones would rub right through. The cushion was just that, a sorry excuse for a mattress, like a gurney used to cart people around at the hospital. Living at the nursing home, she would never again lay on a mattress so thick it would develop a shallow spot where her body would fit into perfectly like a mold.

Since her arrival to the nursing home she slept increasingly more than she was awake. It had started out as boredom and then the stroke had sapped any energy she had left. First she felt the strength leave her muscles where she needed help getting out of bed and then the weakened thumping of her heart and the breaths of air holding less and less oxygen required her to rest before taking the fourteen steps needed to walk to the toilet. She was not getting better. Her body was ready to die. She was ready to die.

'*Am I?*' she questioned herself. '*I have to be.*' Her body would not hold out even if she was determined to find the meaning of her life, any meaning, anything. She did not worry so much about the inevitable looming; she just knew she did not want to be alone. Forgotten.

It felt like she had already been taken out of life's happenings in the world and confined to the four walls she shared with a woman whose mind was gone but body would not die. Her roommate, Lillian, spent most of her waking time grunting, as if in pain. Again and again, like the ticking of a clock came the grunts from the other side of the room, the capacity to communicate with words long gone. A chance to make new friends, Laura's daughter, Karen, had said about moving into the nursing home. But who makes friends in the asylum, Laura thought dryly. Her critical eye had been clouded with tears when she was escorted to her room for the first time which would be not only her new, but last home. Her nerves jangled with the never ending sounds from the hall, the phones ringing at the nurse's station and the pans clanging in the kitchen and sad, weakened voices chanting requests that could not be understood. Her stomach had knotted at the unappealing aroma of institutional food wafting her way. There was something about the mashed potatoes and gravy being delivered to the bed ridden that was putrid smelling, making her nauseous. The distinctive fumes of bleach seemed to seep out of the pale green paint on the walls and the outdated teal colored Naugahyde furniture. She questioned how one could be happy in this environment, working or residing. Maybe they just get use to it, she thought.

Karen was sure the nursing home was the best for her. '*Best for Karen,*' Laura thought and then bit her lip to think ill of her daughter. For as long as she could remember, they seemed to struggle constantly with Karen trying to reverse the parent-child roles. Karen was no longer a child and Laura was parent by title only. She knew Karen had decided on the nursing home with the best intentions, but it felt like convenience to Laura. Karen lived three hours away and argued that it was too far for her to take care of her. Laura was unsure of what this entailed. She had taken care of herself for years and had taken care of Karen, raising her with her own two hands, for that matter. But Karen had garnered her brother, Sam's support after the doctors diagnosed Laura's mini-strokes.

TIA's, transient ischemic attacks, the doctors called them. She never even noticed it had happened. Laura had still been functional, only just a bit forgetful. But who doesn't forget a few things when they get old. Strokes laid people out or made them half a person.

In the confines of the nursing home Laura felt her independence end more and more. Good intended nursing aides would tell her "I'll do that for you," "why don't you wear a sweater today," and "meatloaf and mash potatoes for dinner tonight." Laura felt like she did not have to think anymore when all her decisions were made for her. Walking outside was forbidden unless you were with family. Walking the halls just to stretch her legs met with comments from the aides like "good morning, Laura. Can't you find your room?" But then a real stroke happened and weakened her left side to worthlessness and scrambled her thoughts. Perhaps her daughter was right.

Laura tried not to be bitter. She knew her body was dying. It made her morose to think all her memories would cease and the memories others had of her would eventually too. It was silly to be worried about others forgetting her when it was she who was forgetting things about herself. When Karen had bragged to one of the aides that Laura had been quite an avid knitter, the aide had gone out of her way to find some needles and yarn. The only thing Laura was able to make was a knotted mess. It was silly, but after a while of fussing with it, trying to make it feel right in her hands and begging her fingers to remember how, she wept. The aide tried to console her while apologizing over and over and quietly took it with her when she left the room. Laura was afraid the tangles of the multi colors, dizzying to keep looking at, would tie her fingers up, wrapping around and around until she was shackled like her memory had become.

Hour after hour passed into each other while day took turns with night and the shifts of the nursing aides blended together. Visits from Karen or Sam were too far in between to use as landmarks on the calendar hanging on the bulletin board fastened to the painted cement block wall opposite her bed. The squares of each day remained blank except for the preprinted holidays and remembrances that came to mean nothing other than the seasons continued to pass. No longer did her presence have importance to the rest of the world. Going to the grocery store for milk, depositing a check at the bank or even washing her own clothes and making her own meals had become chores that could be accomplished without her.

Laura tried to figure out which day today was on the calendar. If it was the weekend, Sam might visit. Karen had visited last and Sam visited when he could. He was so much like his father, she was almost glad to see him leave because of his argumentative demeanor. But his wife, Sarah, she was like a breath of fresh air. There was a kindness and gentleness she gave off, a warmth emitted from her dark skin and dark eyes. Laura admired how Sarah presented herself, not having to prove that she was someone or something that she was not, quite unlike Sam's ex-wife. She felt shameful for using Sarah to flaunt her convictions in her husband's face when he was alive. Perhaps she was no better than him because it could have hurt Sarah so much. Maybe Sarah was such a good person she could forgive Laura her faults. She could only hope.

For Laura, the visits could not last long enough. She savored them, holding on to the moment as long as possible, like a square of chocolate held between her tongue and the roof of her mouth until it dissipated into a memory. She craved the sweetness of the visits in between the bland of waiting for the next meal, med pass or inane activity. Laura watched the other residents, some who wept as if time had eroded any composure of emotion or the ones who reached out, literally to the outsiders, trying to relate their own memories conjured, trying to make a connection with another human being. Laura could not cheapen her memories like that. They were something special to her, a part of her life she wanted to give to someone important, wanting to know the memories would be respected and protected. Logically, it was her daughter who was deserving, like any other inheritance, but Karen discounted them, brushing them aside as used and old.

With the seasoned staff worn out from repeated stories, the outside people could be easy targets like the woman who came and sang patriotic songs every Friday afternoon or other people's visitors such as Lillian's daughter who ended up spending hours at the nursing home because she couldn't help but be generous with those starved for attention. It was the most pathetic and vain attempts to merely validate that they were more than aged relics of the past, more than the decaying flesh covered with wrinkly skin and white hair they currently resided within. But sadder yet, were those who had given up trying to prove they were anything else other than 'residents' to the staff within weeks of moving into their new home.

Before the stroke, Sarah would occasionally come alone to visit Laura. Sarah's visits were the most deliciously sweet. Conversely, Laura knew by Karen's nervous energy, she could not wait to leave, as if trying to accomplish enough to be granted freedom back to her life outside the walls of the nursing home. Laura was sure Karen was concentrating on the relief of leaving when the visit came to an end, but Karen was like a lot of the other grown adult children making obligatory visits. Love from those children was gone or on hold during the last months or years of death refusing to come quickly for some of their mothers and fathers. But it was not like the old, frail and senile were encouraged to see their own reflections in the institutional mirrors above the square porcelain sinks that were for washing hands with liquid soap from a dispenser attached to the wall. If only they could forget who they had become.

Of the stories she let spin around and around in her head while she lay in bed waiting for time to pass, she would piece Sarah's visit together in her head. If she imagined hard enough she could feel the warmth of Sarah's hand against her own. She remembered the exaggerated contrast of Sarah's dark skin against her own pale skin that never darkened under the overhead fluorescent lights.

"Your son doesn't mind if I take time out for you," Sarah giggled and leaned over to kiss Laura on the forehead.

"I've been thinking about my grandmother's maiden name and I just can't remember it." Laura's forehead wrinkled as if it could massage her mind into remembering. Laura had been flattered when Sarah had become interested in Sam's family history. Sarah tried to get as much information and stories from Laura as she could. Now, it was crucial for Laura to remember any details as her health continued to fail.

"Julia...Julia..." A few false starts to a name that she knew but could not remember. "She always acted like she felt out of place. The only time she smiled was when she was talking about being in New York. She never got over it. I'm sure she knew that she would never see it again before she died. It had to be a hard life as a pioneer and frontiersman.

She and her family had all the luxuries that you could imagine when she was growing up."

"Don't worry too much about it," Sarah said, pulling back a lock of dark brown hair that had escaped her ponytail. "I found a Julia married to a James Heywood. It's so close to the Harwood listed in your notes."

"Did you check the family bible?" Laura rubbed her temples as she recalled Karen discouraging her from taking the family bible with her to the nursing home. "I think the girl has it."

"Do you mean Karen? I borrowed it from her. It's the embossed brown covered one, right?

"Yes, it was brown." Laura confirmed as more memories were triggered. "My mother use to keep it in her bedroom. When I was little, I use to sneak in and run my fingertips over the raised flowers and leaves that were on it."

"Can you tell me more about your grandmother?"

Laura thought for a moment. "She was good to me, but I think she was unhappy about things that never were."

"What do you mean by that?"

"She longed to go back to New York. She would tell me of the parties she would go to and the dresses she would wear. She talked about riding in the shiny black carriages pulled by beautifully groomed horses when she was little and living in New York, but then riding in a wagon behind work horses when her parents moved to Michigan. She always seemed preoccupied like she was missing something. I think she died very bitter because she longed for the days when there had been money. She knew she was going to die poor. That had to be very hard on her."

"You told me her parents brought her here after they had lost some land?"

"Apparently her father was deep into gambling and booze. Her mother begged her father to stop before he ruined them. When he lost their land due to gambling debts, he thought if he moved the family to Michigan they could start over. There was a railroad boom going through northern Michigan for the lumber desperately needed to rebuild Chicago after the fire. I guess life never got that bad again, but he still squandered any savings that they could have had."

"But why didn't she go back to New York when she grew up?"

"She met and married my grandfather, Levi, and had two little babies before she was twenty-two. I guess that kept her here. I think Grandfather ended up taking the blame for what she never got."

"You're looking tired, Laura," Sarah said.

"It's okay, dear. I like to talk about them. It's my way of keeping them alive." Laura felt the satisfaction of offering food for thought, nourishing Sarah's hungry soul when she shared her memories with her, but it was easy to be generous with Sarah who was so appreciative.

They sat in silence for a few moments and Laura closed her tired eyes. The blood had flowed away, making the skin around her eyes pale white. The lids were void of any color that imitated vitality, leaving a fine powder of age, hazing closer and closer to the mind.

"How did you do it?" Sarah asked softly, as if not meaning for Laura to hear.

"I lived a good life. I worked hard and raised two wonderful children," Laura responded and the skin around her eyes crinkled into upside down smiles.

"I hope I can be your age one day too and not have any regrets," Sarah said hopefully.

Laura mustered a little bit of energy and clasped Sarah's hands. "I do have regrets. Everyone does. If you don't, you haven't lived life."

"If Sam and I had a baby, I wouldn't have any regrets." Laura heard Sarah say and watched her move closer, like Sarah was going to tell her a secret.

"I want to ask you a very personal question," Sarah whispered so close, so intimate, Laura could feel the softness of her voice blow across her face. There was apprehension in the question and Laura could not decide if it was Sarah's or her own, like she had felt with Sarah when they first met.

The image of Sarah disappeared and Laura felt her arm being shook. She tried to hear the question, but could not remember it. Sarah's eyes had been full of forgiveness. The question could not have been bad. Laura's arm was shook again. She opened her eyes and tried to place names with the faces in front of her.

"Hi Mom, Wake up. Do you know who I am?"

"You're that girl," Laura struggled. "The one who grew up with me."

The girl was a woman and looked shocked at what Laura said.

"Mom, it's Karen," the woman said, exasperated. "I'm Karen, your daughter."

"I know that," Laura said, perplexed. She had just forgotten the word daughter.

Laura squinted at Karen and her husband, Mike, like she was in bright sunlight, but there was only the light bar above the head of the bed that dimly illuminated the room and gave a yellowish cast to Laura's white hair. As usual, the blinds to the window were closed.

"Mike came with me today," Karen pressed on with conversation. "It's such a long ride down here that I needed his company to keep me awake."

"How's your business?" Laura addressed Mike with a smile.

"Pretty good. Glad I could take the day off to come visit," he replied.

Karen cut back in. "Has anyone been here to see you this week?"

"Sarah was here a little bit ago," Laura said not sure if she was mixing up the past with the present.

Karen stiffened, as if saddened that her mother was able to identify her brother's wife by name and not her.

"That's nice Mom. Anyone else?"

Laura smiled and her eyes turned into the distinctive upside down smiles. "My mother was here."

Karen looked taken aback. "Mom, she's dead," she said in an accusing way. "Your mother is dead. You must have been dreaming that."

Laura looked upset. "Well, no one told me that," she said and looked away to the window that was closed to any distraction. She knew her mother was dead, but she could not figure out how she had seen her. Laura knew her words betrayed her and did not dare think that her mind would also.

"Mom, do you know how crazy you sound when you say things like that?" Karen was holding back tears that had formed in the corners of her eyes.

"Do you think you're confusing her with someone else?" Mike asked Laura gently.

"She's doing that on purpose," Karen turned to Mike. "I've told her a hundred times if she got better she could stay with us for a while. If she's acting crazy it doesn't matter how healthy her body gets. I won't be able to put up with that."

Mike grabbed her arm and whispered shh-shh.

"Mom, you've got to get better," Karen begged. "Don't you want to come stay with me? We can finish the five-point-star quilt. You could see the grandkids more."

Laura refused to answer her daughter. She knew she would probably say the wrong thing again. It was one thing to lose her mind, but she was still sensitive to keeping her dignity.

"I'm not going to take care of you like a baby," Karen said bitterly.

Just then a nursing aide came in carrying a covered tray.

"Hello there, Laura," she said very loudly. "It's lunch time. Looks like chicken stew." She set the tray on the movable table and lifted the lid. She took a milk carton out of the pocket of her smock and opened the cardboard box, placing a straw in it before pinching it shut again.

"Better eat up before it gets cold," The attendant said as she stuck a spoon into the stew and stirred it around once.

Mike ended up on the opposite side of the bed as he made room for the attendant. He shuffled back around the bed to Karen.

"Do you think we should grab some lunch too and come back?" He asked.

Karen shook her head yes. She quickly brushed her eyes with the back of her hands.

"We'll be back in about an hour, Mom," her voice quivered as Mike led her out of the room.

Laura watched her daughter go and then pushed the tray away from her. She had no appetite for food. It hurt to hear her daughter say those hurtful things, her own flesh and blood. It was deeper than that. Laura felt she had constantly fought Karen to maintain her position as her mother and now she had no choice but to change rolls and let Karen be her parent. There was something scary about becoming a mere shell of herself.

She tried to cheer herself up by thinking about the woman Karen had grown up to be. Karen prided herself in looking younger than she was. She had kept herself up over the years and reveled when someone would refer to her as Sam's little sister. Mike played up her pride and referred to her as his younger wife. Only by one month, whereas he looked his age, with salt and pepper hair, heavily defined wrinkles when he smiled and glasses that seemed to get thicker each year.

Thinking about Karen's tirade wore her out. Laura resigned to herself that she would only regain her youthful energy in her mind for the time while she dreamed. *"I want to ask you a very personal question,"* she could hear Sarah say. It was frustrating to her that she could not remember what Sarah had asked. Maybe the dream would come to her again, like the dreams of the past where she had truly been alive.

CHAPTER 2

On the eve of the move to the nursing home, Laura had stood in the living-room of her home and surveyed the boxes around her. These were the things for the yard sale that Karen had deemed not necessary for her mother to have any longer. The dining room was full of things that Karen or Sam would take to their homes. Laura's bedroom housed a few boxes she would take with her to the nursing home. There was only room for the bare necessities, such as underwear and socks with her name written on each of them with permanent marker.

She had always made a point to wash underwear in hot water, to kill any germs that might be lurking in them. Now her underwear would be washed with all kinds of stranger's underwear. Heaven only knew if the wash cloths she would use to wash her face with would be washed in the same load of some stranger's underwear.

This had been the home where she and her husband raised their children. She had sorted her husband's belongings after his death and she passed on some of his possessions to the children. It was her turn, with the help of Karen, to sort her own things. As much as Laura wished her husband had gotten rid of some of his things which seemed pretty useless in her mind, she was thankful to sort through it after he was dead. It was another chance to touch a part of him and inhale the faint scent of him that permeated his things. She wondered what her children would have to remember her by when they would have to sort through her fleeting possessions at the nursing home.

In a way, it felt like death, even though her body was still very much alive. This was her own death, looming in the near future, reminded by the ticking clock on the mantle and being forced to contemplate that each second brought her closer. What else would you call it, Laura thought, when the children felt it was time for her to reside in a nursing home. The last trip to the doctor for a physical blossomed into several tests which revealed she had suffered a few mini strokes. She marveled at the idea that she was suffering from these, but did not seem to feel it. It was her heart, she knew, that slowed her down. She figured something that rattled around for over seventy years was liable to have worn parts. Laura was certain the doctors had scared her daughter into believing Laura's body was premeditating her death by way of starving her brain.

Laura really wanted to continue living in her home, surrounded by the things she loved. She knew when she died, she would be dead, end of story. She did not want any heroics to bring her back from the dead. The idea of being stuck with needles and tubes shoved in her nose or down her throat did not equate with a good quality of life. Karen tried to guilt trip her into staying alive for as long as possible. For what, Laura could only imagine, maybe to enjoy her possessions a little longer. Yes, she would miss plenty of things. Laura was very sentimental, and almost everything in her house had a story which made the item even more hers. Karen would get short with her and say "you've told me that a hundred times, Mother." It was her daughter-in-law, Sarah, who would follow her around, asking what the story was behind each piece. Almost childlike, Sarah would soak in Laura's stories. She listened to her stories, like when Laura had listened to Grandmother Julia's stories, hanging on to each word as precious.

There had been a few things that could have gone to Karen, or even the yard sale boxes, but Laura had selected them to go to Sarah. She doubted Karen would cherish the things Laura could not take with her to the nursing home. Karen would have no memories attached to the material things of hers. Her daughter-in-law, Sarah, was a bit more sentimental. Some of those things meant something to her, and Laura hoped that they would carry their sentiment then, as Sarah made them a part of her life. The silver plated mirror and hair brush that she had gotten for her sixteenth birthday and the memories surrounding it would be safe with Sarah. When Laura was young, her mother would occasionally brush her hair with it. Her husband brushed her hair with it whenever she was too sick to do it herself. When Karen was little, she would brush Laura's hair, more or less making a mess of it. The hairbrush was not made precious by its usefulness. It was the memories of intimate time with people she loved. Karen had poo-pooed it as being old and junky. The silver was worn in spots and the mirror had become spotty with the silvering coming off in areas.

"That can go in the yard sale box," Karen handed it to Sarah, who was also helping.

"Would you like it?" Laura asked Sarah quietly. "My parents gave me that when I turned sixteen."

"Sure," Sarah said and set it on the bed with a few other things she was taking home.

"Oh, Mom," Karen gushed, lifting a book out of a dresser drawer. "I've been waiting for this."

Laura watched Karen caress the outside of the book. "I'm not dead yet," she said and went to take the book out of Karen's hands.

"You aren't taking this to the nursing home," Karen knitted her eyebrows. "The family bible is too valuable. Anyhow, I'm taking it home and the china doll too."

Laura was surprised at her daughter Karen's assumptions that she should have the family bible and the doll. Usually Karen did not have sentimental feelings about anything. Anything considered old to Karen, was destined for the trash. New was always the best.

"Of course the bible should go to me," Karen stated. "I'm the oldest. Sam won't take care of it anyways."

Laura noticed Sarah bite her lip, most likely wanting to defend her husband from his own sister.

"It's been in the family for a long, long time," Laura commented.

"Yes, and Sam doesn't have kids. At least if I take it, my boys will inherit it," Karen made another point.

These shrouded insults were noticed and Laura watched Sarah turn away from Karen, hiding her anger, hiding her hurt that Laura could see in the tense way she held herself.

"Nobody's arguing with you, Karen," Sarah said with her back turned and pushing things around in a cardboard box like she was busy. "But I don't think having kids makes one more family or not."

"Well, I guess if you're going to take care of it," Laura acquiesced.

"How did this doll get a crack in its head?" Sarah asked, picking up the aged doll from its home on the rocking chair.

"I'm not sure. It was my Grandmother Julia's from when she was a little girl. I'm sure she was loved by lots of little girls."

"I thought you said your grandmother always had her sitting on her dressing table?" Karen questioned.

"I guess she did," Laura admitted and thought about how she had asked Grandmother Julia how the doll had gotten broken. She was never told, but had a suspicion that her mother had broken it. Her mother had looked so sad that day in Grandmother Julia's bedroom.

"This was your Grandmother Julia's doll?" Sarah asked.

Laura made her way over to Sarah. A big smile washed over Laura's face with her eyes making upside down smiles.

"This china doll made it all the way from France to the big city of New York and finally to the wilderness of northern Michigan. It's hard to believe she made it when her hands and feet and face are as fragile as a china tea cup. Grandmother Julia would allow me to sit on her bed and hold the doll." Laura smoothed out the doll's silky dress the color of faded rose petals and trimmed in lace the color of old paper. She stroked the fine yellow hair that framed a painted-on face of blue eyes with delicate black eyelashes and blood red lips. "While sitting on Grandmother Julia's bed, she would tell me stories of New York when she was a little girl. My favorite story was about the money hidden in New York. Grandmother Julia would become animated and a glint of happiness would be caught in her eyes."

"Was it ever found?" Sarah asked.

Karen snorted, "Can't find what isn't there. I think Grand-mother Julia wished there was lost money."

"It was very real and very important to Grandmother Julia," Laura defended.

"Well, the bible and the doll are the only things I really care about," Karen reaffirmed.

"Anything you don't take to the nursing home can go to the yard sale."

That made Laura wonder if it was okay to feel sad about her material possessions, even if they were trivial. The metal ice cream scoop that made many a child smile when they saw her take it out of the kitchen drawer. The silky pillow case, now threadbare, that Karen and Sam had fought over to have on their bed when they were children. Karen had held it up between her fingers and wrinkled her nose at it while exclaiming "Why do you keep such rags?"

"Because it means something to me," Laura retorted.

"The only thing it means is you are a packrat. If it's old, throw it out. That's my motto."

"Obviously, I must have spoiled you growing up."

Karen gave a bitter laugh. "Mom, I only remember everything being worn when I was growing up. Furniture, clothes, cars and that kitchen table with the wobbly legs. What's the point of keeping something that's old and outdated. Like this," she held up a tattered baby quilt. "It's useless and shabby."

"Not to me."

"I guess that's the difference between you and me," Karen sighed. "I love the smell of new cars, new clothes, leather, clothes from the dry cleaners..."

"I don't think of it as keeping rags." Laura bit her lip to keep from crying as Karen ridiculed her. She wondered if the nursing home was where people put the old and fragile because it would be too crass to throw them away. For no other reason than being old, Laura was giving up the things that had been important to her. She did not bother to make Karen understand, one more time, that she was keeping memories.

CHAPTER 3

At the age of twenty eight, Laura had the energy to keep the house, do the farm chores and take care of the children. The hard work had made the muscles in her arms and legs bulge sinuously. Her belly was betraying though, unable to hide that she would be a mother again.

She loved the sunshine and working in its warmth. It made her feel alive. Eventually it would catch up and mar her skin with wrinkles and age spots, disguising her youthful soul that resisted feeling older.

Before she met her husband, Peter, she was vibrant and lithe. Her muscles, limbered up with farm chores, lay smooth, under her taut skin, like a creamy white sheet pulled across the bed. She had been told she resembled her Grandmother Julia, a true beauty who others used to measure all others against. But when she realized her looks began to get her attention from others outside of her family, she sought more of it. It became a game for her, to compare herself against the other girls and then tease the young men that they could have her, but only if she wanted them to.

Perhaps in the sanctity a church, her attendance based on a friend's invitation rather than devotion, Laura's wild regard for others was halted the moment she looked into Peter's icy blue eyes. He smiled so broadly and professed that he wanted to marry her and have children and raise them with God's word. In the orbs of his eyes there was an endless sky that could be her world that he had invited her to come share. With his sandy blond hair slicked back into place, who could not believe what he said as she fell into the curving embrace of his smile.

Such stability, such goodness, Laura could not resist. And there would be children who would love her back. Memories of when her brothers Harry and Little Andrew were alive whetted her craving for her own family. After their deaths she had become an only child and she did not like it. She had been so lonely without them, compounded with her mother's continual detachment and her father's drunken bouts that led him down the path to other women's beds.

She and Peter would live right. He was a hard worker and was driven about farming. She would bear him children and create a loving home. She stopped using her looks to play games with others and was determined to make her marriage fulfilling for both of them as she took her commitment to her husband seriously and worked hard.

Sitting on the front porch, she worked on knitting a heavy wool sock for Peter. He liked to wear them while hunting in the winter. The grey wool twined between her fingers and grew into an increasingly darker shade as dusk began to fall. She had to keep reminding herself to let the yarn travel loosely from her fingers to the needles. Ordinarily, knitting was a mindless diversion for her hands, but tonight her mind was taut with anger at her husband. Over dinner, she let the muscles in her mouth chew the food instead of confronting him. She made no show to Peter that she knew his secret plans for the evening. It was Peter's secret only to her, while to everyone else in the county it was a common fact, as uttered from the crude lips of the neighbor woman. He had avoided lying to her by neglecting to tell her where he was really going. She clamped down on the thoughts and forced them to simmer in the back of her mind, imagining how she would serve them to him when he returned.

The spring peepers chirped loudly, filling the silence in between Karen and Sam's chatter. They tromped back and forth across the clumps of patchy grass of new blades with the roots working to fill in the bare spots.

"Come on, Sam," Karen said with exasperation. "We're playing school."

"I don't want to," he said, squatting on his haunches and poking at the dirt with his fingers.

"Don't you want to get smart?" Karen stood with her hands on her hips.

"I am smart."

"What's the capitol of Nebraska?"

"I said I'm not playing school."

"How come you have to be so difficult?"

Laura cleared her throat. "Sam, why don't you come up here with me?"

"No. I'm playing with Karen."

"But she's picking at you."

"I don't care."

Laura shook her head. Her baby, her son and all he wanted was his sister.

"Karen, Sam," Laura called to her children and stood up. "It's time to go in."

"Com'on Sam. It's time for you to go in," Karen echoed to her little brother.

The three of them made their way into the dark house. Laura turned on the light in the bathroom and took a clean cloth and dampened it under the faucet.

"You first, Karen," Laura called her over to her. She washed her face and neck, then her hands. Not only was her temperament like her father's, but when her eyes flashed with impudence, Laura dared to not look away.

"It's your turn Sam," Laura said.

"I want Karen to do it," he asserted.

"I will do it," Laura said between clenched teeth. "I'm you mother.

Karen steered Sam towards their mother.

Laura washed Sam's face that was streaked from sweat running down his dusty face. After cleaning him up, she helped them undress and wiggle into nightshirts.

"Let's say our prayers," Karen directed Sam. He giggled and dove into the bed.

"Come on, Sam," Laura cajoled.

Karen stood in her usual stance with her hands on her hips, glaring at her little brother. "You need to say your prayers or you'll go to Hell."

"Karen," Laura admonished.

"Daddy said so," Karen defended.

"Both of you say your prayers," Laura instructed. They kneeled at the side of the bed and clasped their hands in front of themselves.

They finished the Lord's Prayer and Laura lifted Sam back into his bed and he slid in between the cool sheets.

"Good night Sam," Laura kissed him. "I love you."

Karen bent over her little brother and kissed him too. "Good night. I love you, Sam."

Laura rolled her eyes at Karen's little mother routine. Karen was only eight and she had taken Sam for her own. If Sam wanted a story or hurt himself, he wanted Karen. Laura wished Sam would want her sometimes.

Laura helped Karen into her bed next to Sam's and kissed her goodnight. She pulled the quilt that her mother had made from all of her dresses she outgrew as a child, up to Karen's chin.

The window had been open during the day, letting the fresh air inside. With dusk settling, the air had become chilly, so Laura closed the window until there was only a crack, muffling the chorus of peepers outside and the earthy musky smell of spring.

It had been a long day for Laura and she slumped into the rocking chair in her bedroom. She felt twinges of a baby growing, the familiar feelings of life surging through her bones and through her soul. She would love this baby like her other two and raise this child to work hard and treat others fairly, regardless of how they looked. Peter would probably teach this child to fear God and quote from the Bible like he had with Sam and Karen. The little faith Laura had for religion was squelched almost to nothing when Peter insisted that God's word gave him superiority over others and the power to judge them. He had a book and made logic from it. Laura had her heart and felt he was wrong. Regardless, she had to respect her husband. He was a good provider and protector of their family.

After witnessing her own mother's humiliation of her father's infidelity, Laura was compelled to support her husband no matter what, as long as he remained faithful to her. Faithfulness in marriage or religion though, was not enough for Laura to keep her opinion to herself. The idea that Peter loved a wrathful and judging God contradicted her ideals of a tolerant Jesus. It gave her strength when she thought about confronting Peter when he came home from the meeting. She knew tonight she would not mince her words, but state how she felt. She fell asleep as she waited patiently for him to come home. The rocking had calmed her anger just as it had soothed the children to sleep while cradled in her arms so many times before.

It was past midnight when she was awakened by the headlights shining through the bedroom window. Laura went to the kitchen and met Peter entering the back door. He looked tired. He took his hat off and a few curls had been released from below where the sweat and grime had flattened his hair against his head.

"Would you like something to eat?" Laura asked, already getting a plate out of the cupboard.

"A little something would be okay," Peter answered, guarded, looking at her out of the corner of his eyes. "What are you still doing up?"

"I guess there was something that I wanted to talk to you about and didn't get the chance to during dinner."

Peter stayed quiet while Laura slathered butter on two pieces of bread and put a thick slice of roast beef in the middle of it.

Peter took a bite and chewed it, finishing with a slurp of milk that Laura had also set in front of him.

"What did you want to talk about?" He asked and took another bite.

"Rose Nelson was here this afternoon. She asked if you were going to the meeting tonight."

Peter swallowed his bite hard.

"What did you say to her?" He asked.

"I told her you were planning on going to see Nestor," she informed him as she folded her arms in front of her. "I wasn't sure about any meeting. I asked her what kind of meeting she was talking about."

Peter quit eating and was sitting back in his chair. He looked at his plate. He didn't respond to her so she continued.

"I tolerate Rose because she's a neighbor, but it was really hard for me to do even that when she narrowed her beady eyes and said 'you know, that meetin' at the fairground 'bout niggers. We can't have 'em runnin' round these parts ruinin' things for us honest folk," she mimicked the clipped way Rose seemed to bite her words, half chewed and spewing out of her mouth.

Peter showed no emotion but stared at the half eaten sandwich.

"If I hadn't been so mad, I would have laughed in her face. Judging people she doesn't even know and her brother is in jail for stealing. Everyone knows the reason her husband's not in jail is because he's smarter than her brother."

"Is that all?" Peter asked and then returned to eating the sandwich.

"Don't you think you should be honest with your wife?"

Peter chewed slowly and finally answered. "I did go to Nestor's."

"And I assume you both went to the meeting?"

Peter didn't answer her.

"Well?" Laura said firmly.

"You don't understand this Laura."

"I don't understand? There's only one Negro family for a hundred miles in any direction from here. Have they committed a crime that they need an entire community to run them off? We don't know them and they don't know us. Can't we keep it that way? They aren't bothering anyone." Laura put Peter's plate in the sink, daring to waste the food still on it. His silence made her angry.

"What are you thinking Peter?" Whirling around, she lashed out at Peter. "Getting our family involved with these kind of people. These people that hate and control by fear. They're just cowards hiding their faces under white sheets."

"You don't understand. I'm doing this to protect our family."

"Protect us from what Peter?"

"I can't say no. If I do I endanger our family."

"Oh pshaw. The only thing you are doing is providing a poor example for our children," Laura said, wiping the crumbs on the table in front of Peter. "I know you won't change the way you feel, but you promised me you wouldn't be so public about your prejudice."

"Laura, the Klan is a stronger force here in the north than in the south. They just get more publicity down there."

"How is that important to our family?"

"Because if you aren't with them, they feel you are against them."

"Peter, I married you because I thought that you believed in the right things. Because I thought you would be a good husband and provider. Because I thought you would be a good father. Because you would protect us. Now I don't know who you are."

"I'm doing all of that. I haven't changed," Peter stood up and the chair legs scraped against the worn wooden floor. He held onto the back of the chair as if for support. "You don't understand. It's true, I don't like niggers and I have no use for them. But the real reason I'm doing it is because I'm afraid of what could happen to my family. I fear for my family. This is the only way I know how to protect them."

Laura looked at Peter stone faced.

"I'm sorry if you regret marrying me Laura. I'm doing this because I love you and I love my children." Peter left the room.

Laura stood at the kitchen sink and sobbed as she heard Peter creep into the children's room and kiss them both goodnight. She felt guilty thinking about raising another child under Peter's hateful thoughts. She could have refused to share her life with Peter when she found out he hated blacks and

Indians and communist Japs, but that would have meant leaving him while her first born grew inside her.

She remembered how the world that encompassed her life felt like it had shattered when Peter told her the story of his uncle's father bringing slaves with him to Michigan.

"You're making that up," Laura had said incredulously.

"No, it's true."

"Oh, those poor people."

"What are you talking about?" Peter huffed and pointed at the dilapidated house that looked like a pile of boards propped up. "Look at the way they live. They live like animals."

"That's not nice," she willfully corrected him.

"You're right," he grinned deviously. "If Uncle George hadn't brought niggers here in the first place they wouldn't be making an eyesore on the land now."

"I can't believe you're saying that. I'm not going to raise my child to think like that."

"They're an inferior race," Peter tried to reason with Laura. "Them and the injuns. How could they shun being Christians for thousands of years? They aren't God's chosen."

"I'm not raising my child to think like that." Laura's eyes squinted hard underneath her furrowed brow. Happiness did not come from the upside down smiles of her eyes. Fire seeped from them.

"I'm not raising my child to think like that," she dared to repeat in her mind as she looked out the kitchen window and stared at the reflection of herself against the darkness of the night. She was not raising her child to hate negroes. She was going to raise three.

CHAPTER 4

Laura woke and pulled the covers closer to her face. The air was crisp in her bedroom. Today felt like a special day. She searched her mind trying to think why, other than it was Saturday and no school. That was celebration enough for seventeen year old Laura.

She heard the cook stove door squeak open. Mother had shuffled into the kitchen and was probably putting a log onto the anemic bed of coals. The back door banged closed. Harry had gone out to do chores.

Laura slid out of the warmth of her bed and quickly dressed in a sweater and an old pair of her brothers dungarees. She breezed into the kitchen where her mother was measuring flour into a big bowl.

"I'm going to feed the chickens," Laura told her as she grabbed the egg basket off the hook by the door. The ground crunched under her feet as she walked to the chicken coop. Lake effect snow floated lazily in the air like milkweed down. She spread feed around the pen and pumped fresh water to pour into their shallow bowls. Stepping up into the coop, she cautiously slid her hands under the golden colored bellies of the Buff Orphingtons sitting on their nests. Light brown eggs filled the bottom of the basket.

Laura walked to the barn and waited for Harry to finish his chores so they could walk back to the house together. Harry usually kidded around with her, but this morning he was pensive. Back inside the house, Laura set the eggs down on the counter. Mother had just set down a plate of hotcakes on the table where Father sat bleary eyed and with a cup of coffee grasped between his hands. Harry and Father served themselves hotcakes and thick slices of ham, and started eating.

"My coffee's empty, Rose," Father said. Mother got up and filled his cup with more black liquid that turned brown as it mixed with the milk he had poured in.

Mother went back to washing dishes.

"Mother," Laura called. "Come sit and eat."

Laura noticed her mother's hand going to her face as if to brush something away. Slowly, she turned around and wiped her hands dry on her apron. Her face looked old and tired.

"Are you going hunting Harry?" Laura asked, hoping he might not and instead go horseback riding with her.

"Yes. Father and I talked about going out after breakfast," he replied.

Laura watched her mother staring into her cup of coffee. She looked up at Laura and cleared her throat.

"Are you going to be home for dinner Harry?" Mother smiled, contradicting her sad eyes. "Or are you going into town with Claire?"

"I dunno," Harry mumbled with syrupy hotcake filling his mouth. "I haven't talked to her yet."

"She's a nice girl," Mother mused, still not filling her plate.

"Emma said Claire is waiting for you to ask her," Laura blurt out, referring to her friend who was Claire's younger sister.

"Laura," her father scolded.

Laura was becoming impatient with her family. They all seemed to be going through the motions of the day without any excitement. She was determined to have some fun.

"Is anything happening today?" Laura asked, still sure that the day had more significance than just being a weekend day.

"Today's Little Andrew's birthday," Mother said quietly.

Laura looked down at her plate ashamed. Little Andrew. She had forgotten. They had stopped having celebrations and birthday cake and presents eight years ago when he died.

"I'll be home for dinner," Harry said gruffly.

Harry and Father finished breakfast and started making their way out, while Mother still held her coffee mug between her hands. Laura made sandwiches for Harry and her father and got apples out of the cellar.

They came back to get the guns and Father filled his flask full of whisky.

"This will keep me warm," he winked at Laura. She tried to smile, but despair filled her throat, paralyzing the words she was not even sure she knew the names of to describe her feelings. Laura cleared the table silently.

"See you later, old girl," Father gingerly touched Mother's arm as he walked past her to go out.

Laura bent her head down and concentrated on washing the dishes. When she looked up she noticed they had forgotten their lunches. She ran out after them. She caught up to Harry and threw her arms around him. He stopped and turned around in her embrace and hugged her back.

"It's okay, Laura," he said, nuzzling the top of her head. "Take care of Mother this morning. I'll be back later this afternoon." He ambled off toward his father.

Laura was not worried about Mother. She always survived Little Andrew's birthday. Laura was more worried about Harry. She knew he had spent a lot of time at the lake. His mind was too preoccupied with Little Andrew. She watched Harry in his red and black Mackinaw jacket, thinking he was so handsome. All the young girls pined over him. She knew he would not marry

Claire, just like the other girls who had allowed him to court them. He was too afraid to let anyone get close to him. Laura knew he blamed himself for not saving Little Andrew. She wanted to tell him again it was not his fault he did not save Little Andrew. They had all told him that, but he refused to believe it.

Laura remembered the day at the big lake. Little Andrew had been seven. Harry almost drowned trying to save him. She had been playing on the beach and had been unaware of what was happening. All she remembered was leaving the beach early and Mother holding Little Andrew wrapped in blankets on the way home. It was as if he was sleeping cradled in her arms. Laura had loved Little Andrew and his death was not real for quite a while for her. She bitterly thought how the occasion of his funeral was fun. It was like Christmastime without the presents, when all of her cousins, aunts and uncles came.

After the funeral, all the cousins went home. There was just the four of them, no longer five. A quietness settled over the house and Laura became lonely for Little Andrew. Harry slunk around with guilt harnessed to his soul. Mother would sneak off to cry while Father kept company with his bottle of amber comfort. Little Andrew may have been gone, but Laura felt the rest of her family was out of reach and no one to share being alive with her.

'Take care of Mother,' Laura thought bitterly. 'Don't forget about me. Don't forget I miss Little

Andrew too.' She stood in the yard and watched her father and Harry become specks in the distance as they crossed the field.

CHAPTER 5

'Don't forget me,' Laura woke thinking. She was transported from the farm in her dream back to the monotony of the nursing home. A few bits of light coming through the slats of the aluminum blinds on the window freckled her face. The overhead light had been turned on while Laura ate breakfast, but the attendant turned it off when she returned for the barely touched breakfast tray. It was most likely done with the attendants best intentions as Laura's eyes were closed at that time. The blinds stayed closed, allowing the world outside to seemingly continue on without her.

Laura dozed on and off, occasionally hearing a bird chirping, by chance outside her window and not in her mind. She kept trying to remember the question Sarah had asked her. More importantly she wanted to remember what answer she had given to her daughter-in-law. How could she forget?

In that limbo state of sleep Laura suddenly felt that someone was in her room. She opened her eyes. At first it seemed like a shadow, but as her eyes focused she saw her mother.

Her mother lifted a finger to her lips and smiled.

Laura whispered. "I'm ready, Mother."

Rose shook her head back and forth a few times.

"I'm sorry Laura, but that is not my choice," she said and touched Laura's hand. "But I'll be with you. You won't be alone."

"I just hope I have enough energy..." Laura trailed off, already exhausted.

"Don't worry about that. You may be tired and weak now, but once you are back with us you will not know those words again."

"Thank you, Mother," Laura mustered, barely audible. It comforted Laura to have her mother there. She had forever fantasized that her mother would be there for her, not necessarily in death, but all the times in her life when she sought her mother's reassurance and acceptance. Despite all of the things Laura tried to do, it had never changed her mother's distance from her. Maybe her mother really did not like her, but Laura knew if she kept trying, eventually she could get her mother to love her. Her mother had never been mean or treated her poorly, she just was not affectionate with Laura like she was with Harry or Little Andrew.

While it felt like her mother had been neglectful, seemingly by choice, her father was just someone you could not get close to. As a child, Laura figured, one grows up knowing and taking for granted that their parents are Mother and

Father, separate entities who orbit in the same house. It was not until she was much older that Laura contemplated her parent's relationship with each other. It was hard to imagine a young James and an even younger Rose deciding to marry and have a family. Father standing a bit shorter next to Mother who always looked like she was trying to hide, unsure of herself, ashamed and never explaining the scar across her nose. It was incongruous to think they stayed married and were life partners when they did not seem to be deeply attached to each other, but maybe the connection had been Little Andrew and Harry. Perhaps she had been too young to see her parent's intimate relationship when Little Andrew and Harry were alive and how it held her parents together.

Her mother taught her how to cook and clean and knit socks, everything she would need to be a successful housewife. Her mother constantly reminded her that the way a person looks means nothing, it's what was inside them that determined if they were a good person or not. These were all lessons her mother had passed down. But the lesson regarding looks had its contradictions.

While struggling with Peter attending the meetings, Laura had sought her mother's advice and not the hurtful words her mother dispensed.

"I don't like Peter being part of a group that is so full of hate. I can't change the way he thinks, but there's no reason why I have to raise my children to think they are better than anyone with a different skin color. What do you think I should do?" Laura had asked her mother.

"I don't know Laura. You're going to have to figure it out yourself." Her mother continued her scrubbing on the pot in the kitchen sink.

Her mother's answer and seemingly lack of interest frustrated Laura. "Sometimes I wish I had never married him. Don't you ever think that about Father?" she challenged her mother.

"Sometimes you have to take everything that's bad, just to have something," her mother stopped scrubbing and looked across the room and glared at her. "You keep looking at what you don't have, Laura, you'll never appreciate what you do have."

"You never appreciated me," Laura charged and took a step towards her mother. "You only wanted Little Andrew and Harry."

"You're like your Grandmother Julia," her mother defensively countered. "She always wanted what she couldn't have and then took it out on those who couldn't give it to her."

"At least I knew Grandmother Julia loved me."

"You don't know anything," her mother's voice strained through her teeth. Her soapy wet hand came up and slapped Laura's cheek that was already burning in anger. "You don't know."

But it was while standing at the edge of her mother's freshly dug grave, Laura felt vindicated. Yes, she had lost a baby, but she still had Karen and

Sam. Her mother had lost Little Andrew and Harry, but never appreciated the daughter who had lived. Laura pitied her parents. She had tried to reach out to them, attempting to make up for the losses of her brothers. They were not the only ones suffering Little Andrew and Harry dying. It hurt and she wanted to stamp her foot at her parents and yell *'I'm still here. I'm your child too. I still need you.'* There was no doubt her mother truly suffered after Little Andrew drowned that summer, so long ago. The whole family suffered the loss, it had not been her mother's alone.

Laura knew what loss was when Little Andrew had died and her father spent the rest of his life drowning himself in whisky and her mother created a boundary around her, defensively distancing herself from everyone around, refusing to even share her grief, like it was hers alone. She knew what loss was when Harry was shot dead during deer hunting season by a hunter from the south who shot at sounds.

Shortly after Laura and her mother's fight, Laura gave birth to her second son. She knew what loss was when his life could only be measured in breaths before dying in her arms. There were no encouraging words from her mother as he struggled to his death. Instead her mother had washed the dishes, cooked the meals for the children and Peter, did the laundry and scrubbed the floors while Laura could not. Laura was grateful for the help but more than anything wanted her mother to acknowledge her pain.

Loss had become familiar as she watched her mother's casket being lowered into the frosty fall ground. *'I need you still,'* Laura wanted to call out to her mother, lying lifeless inside the pine box. She looked at her children, Karen, now twenty, Sam, fifteen. She drew them close into an embrace. As long as she had them, she wanted to believe she would not be alone.

Life had exhausted her and Laura convinced herself she could not be afraid of death. She could not be afraid to question her mother after all those years had passed where she had been unwilling to confront her mother, fearing it would drive her further away. At first, Laura was hesitant, when her mother appeared at her bedside at the nursing home. It felt surreal the first time her mother had come to comfort her, to ease her fears. Before, Mother never seemed to have the time or the ability, as if something held her back from doing it. Laura pushed it out of her head that her mother was making amends. Whether it was appropriate, she was feeling vindicated, her mother would not be lamenting Little Andrew or Harry this time. It would be all about Laura, yearning for her mother to treat her as precious, like her Grandmother Julia always had. Her mother was there and she would not die alone.

CHAPTER 6

For several weeks after Peter died, Laura spent afternoons sorting papers and going through his things. The house felt empty without him. They had managed 'till death do us part for almost forty-five years. She should have felt relieved that the amount of work it took to take care of him the past few years had been alleviated, but it had given her an odd feeling of purpose.

Thankfully Peter's failing capacities were something she could handle and it did not preclude or preempt her from taking care of him until his death. She was sure a move to the nursing home would be the most disturbing thing that could happen to him. A new environment for someone who needed the comfort of the familiar could only heighten his anxieties and fears. Laura committed herself, for as long as she could, to let him know the familiar touch of his favorite coffee mug, know where the bathroom was and let him wake up in the middle of the night in his own bed. She knew the night terrors of waking up, disoriented from deep sleep and the dreadful feeling of not knowing where she was. She still respected Peter as a person and did not want him to wake up confused and still not know where he was after the fog of sleep had lifted. Karen had admonished her, tried to shame her into moving him into the nursing home, "Why won't you let Dad have the necessary care to keep him well? Do you honestly believe he's better off at home?"

Blessed with a lifetime of health, Peter could hardly be concerned with his deteriorating body when sometimes, literally overnight, his memory receded like low tide, and scattered on the wet beach were those little creatures stranded on a foreign space, even though it was still home. Laura watched his old memories become more and more important as if new ones would no longer be made. New experiences of today would have no importance or endurance when tomorrow came, and he would refuse to accept them, be associated or take ownership. Those new memories became stray cats which followed at his heels and he rationalized that they belong to someone else.

She even considered that she took care of Peter out of love, but there was a nagging voice of accusation in her head saying she did it to preserve his secret even though she had disagreed with his hate, could never understand his prejudice.

Karen was worried about her being alone at the farm. She had even nagged at Laura to move in with her even before Peter had died. "After Dad dies, you should move in with us." Laura loved her daughter, but shuddered at the formidable change of roles. She could only imagine being governed by Karen's bossiness. It was hard to believe she found her own child annoying. Laura pondered this as she carried half a dozen boxes outside to the fire pit by the field.

Countless children had spent many a night out by the bonfire. Invariably, the smell of melting rubber always seemed to mix with the smokiness as one child would always take a dare and walk too close to the flames, regardless of how many times the adults gave reminders to back away from the fire. Laura recalled the children roasting hotdogs charred on the outside while still cold in the middle and the countless marshmallows that melted off the sticks before they could be pulled from the fire. Karen's boys loved the fire and begged for one each time they visited.

Laura got a decent fire started and she fed it a handful of loose papers. It caught and started turning the white paper into black thin wafers, crumbling to the bottom of the pit already filled with light grey ashes. She reached into the box and pulled out a folded up piece of white material. Finding an edge, she unfurled it, letting the rest fall to the ground. Between her fists, she grasped the material and started ripping it apart. Her forehead tightly furrowed as if it would aid her ripping the cloth. Piece after piece, she threw it into the fire.

Her husband's robes. How silly to call them that, she thought. They did not keep him warm or give him the air of grandeur or importance that some robes conveyed. They signified hatred and fear. She believed the men hiding behind them were cowards. They refused to show their faces in the process of committing crimes against other humans. Laura could not understand how they could justify violence because of a person's skin color. They thrived and enjoyed the duplicity that the robes provided them. When Laura met them face to face, they were upstanding citizens of the community, good husbands, good fathers, just like Peter had been. They believed the anonymity of the robes gave them immunity to their evil actions.

The last bit of cloth was engulfed in the flames. The physical evidence was gone, but the shame continued. Laura could pretend it never happened, but she knew she would never forget it. The argument with her husband was hers alone and became a secret she would not let the children find out about.

She did not know whether to believe in Peter's spiteful God or if it was her parents half - hearted attempts at teaching her Christianity that made her think this way. Her family's attendance at church had been sporadic. Her father's bouts of drinking often left him in no condition to listen to the pastor pontificate on the sins of poor living. After Little Andrew's death, Mother could occasionally be heard mumbling, "What kind of God would do this?" Laura, not required to attend church on those kind of Sundays, would go off, riding her horse. It was one of those Sundays she had found a rural little church she did not know existed out in the countryside. One would never guess its utility by its rustic exterior, except for the beautiful noises coming from it.

How could God not see the beauty of the women dressed in their best, even if it was shabby, and the children's black skin glowing red from being scrubbed clean and smelling sharp with the smell of home-made lye soap. Or the celebrating sounds swelling out between the clapboards of the church like rainbows as they sang songs, unlike the militant, straight cadence of the hymns at the church she occasionally attended. She was feeling like an outsider and became afraid of being seen, so she hid and watched. She visited often, taking in the sacrament of their music.

As a parent, she wanted to prove to Peter that she could raise the children without thinking of other people belonging to an inferior race. It wasn't that she disliked her own white skin, but could not fathom God favoring his white children over his black. When Laura heard the woman from the negro family which Peter had admonished had been sick, she took Karen and Sam with her to deliver food.

The family lived quietly at the edge of a town that had ceased to exist. Why they did not move south to the cities where there were more like them, was a question the locals asked. The answer was a family secret, Peter's family's secret, who liked to forget his uncle's ancestors had brought their negro ancestors north.

Laura felt her gumption waiver when she drove up to the house and could not find a clear path in the yard that could be considered for parking a car. A handful of scrubby chickens ran across a hard packed yard with nubs of green plucked close to the ground. She figured she had already defied Peter, she might as well go through with disobeying him and pulled up close to the porch. She sounded the horn, announcing her arrival and hoping to rouse the inhabitants.

Standing on that same dilapidated porch Peter had pointed to with disdain, Laura embraced an armload of food. Karen held tight to Sam's hand, refusing to let him explore. Laura was thankful for that as she knocked on the crude jam of the open door. The bare wood, weathered dry, was heavily grooved and silver grey. The windows in Laura's chicken coop were in better condition than the two flanking the doorway, looking blindly out, opaque with dirt.

"Hello, I have some food for you," Laura called into the dark house, not knowing who exactly she was addressing.

A girl Karen's age appeared and took the food into the house and came back for the rest with a little boy tagging behind.

"I hope your mother gets to feeling better," Laura said as gently as she could. "I wish I could do more."

"Thank you, ma'am," the girl whispered.

Karen gawked at the girl, who was even skinnier than she was. She wore no shoes and Karen wrinkle her nose at the impropriety.

"Where are your shoes?" Karen asked her scornfully.

"Don't have any," the girl bowed her head when she answered.

It did not occur to Laura that she did not have shoes. She thought perhaps the girl just wasn't wearing any. It was easy to feel sorry for the girl, but it was not sympathy this girl needed.

"My daddy says you niggers don't have any sense." Karen stood with her one hand on her hip, Sam's hand still clenched in the other.

"Young lady," Laura hollered at her daughter and grabbed her by the arm. "That is no way to talk to anyone. You hear me?"

"You're hurting me," Karen squirmed.

"You take your shoes off," Laura demanded.

"What?"

"Take your shoes off and give them to that girl." Laura shook her daughter as Karen wrestled with her.

"No, Mamma, these are my favorite shoes," Karen wailed. "No Mamma."

Laura wrenched the shoes off her daughter's feet and handed them to the girl.

"Thank you ma'am," the girl said and hung her head shamefully, looking down at her bare feet, not daring to make eye contact with Laura.

"Well, put them on," Laura said exasperated.

The girl shoved her dusty feet into the blue maryjanes with gum soles. Her feet looked lost, barely filling the molded space Karen's feet had created.

Laura brushed the angry tears out of her eyes and looked over at Sam who had walked over to the little boy, oblivious to his mother and sister's ruckus. She watched the little boy with eyes as big and white as the ironstone bowls she ladled chicken and dumplings into. A smile broadened across his face as he looked into Sam's.

"Come on, Sam," Laura voice cracked as she called to him. "It's time to go home."

She loaded her crying daughter into the back seat of the car while Sam crawled onto the front seat with her and stood on it, waving to the little boy with the big toothy smile. Laura glanced back and saw the girl, still looking down at the shoes on her feet.

"Why did you do that?" Karen accused her mother from the back seat.

"We take care of our own," Laura replied.

Peter was not happy when Karen reported her mother's abuses to him.

"How can I protect the family when you advertise like that?" he questioned Laura.

"If you're going to protect us the way you are, I have to at least teach the children some morals."

"Don't accuse me of jeopardizing the family. You're the one doing it."

Almost fifty years later Laura could still feel the heat of his glare, trying to melt her with guilt.

'Please forgive me,' she said to the fire. To God and to her neighbors of color and to humanity, she begged. *'Please forgive my cowardice, by not standing up to him, allowing him to continue even though I knew it was wrong.'*

Laura had tried to love him, but could not forgive him. She had vehemently hid his secret for years, burying it in the far depths of her soul. To break the secret would only cause hurt and heartache. Yet, she wanted everyone to know who her husband really was. But to wish that would expose how her omissions made her guilty. She was no better than her husband or the people he had joined ranks with. Laura's stomach churned at her own duplicity.

Sam and Karen and definitely Sarah would not understand, she reasoned. She did not understand her own irrationality. But Sarah never needed to know.

From the first time Laura met Sarah, she was mesmerized by her light hazel eyes against her dark skin. It was like she could look right through you, deep inside where your feelings hid, where all the knowledge and experiences accumulated. *'Please understand me,'* Laura begged with her own eyes.

At the time she had been draining the heavy pot of potatoes she had made for mashed potatoes and gravy and roast chicken. She saw Sam's car pull up in the drive. Her hands full, she knew she would never beat Karen to the door to greet Sam and his new girlfriend. Laura continued working on the potatoes as she listened for Sam's voice, over the football game Peter was watching in the other room with Mike and the grandsons. Watching through his eyelids, she grumbled, thinking about every time she went to turn the volume down, his eyes would jump open and he would say 'I'm watching that.'

Karen and Sam made it into the kitchen with his new girlfriend tagging behind.

"Hi Mom," he kissed Laura on the cheek. "This is Sarah."

Laura stared at the woman behind Sam. Corkscrew curls hung stiff around her face. Big round eyes looked out over apple shaped cheeks. The curves of her body echoed more roundness which Laura wanted to touch, tracing the surfaces.

Laura put the potato masher down. "Sarah, I'm so glad you're here."

"Thank you," she replied quietly as the volume of Karen's voice had taken over in conversation with Sam. Sam drifted into the dining room to nibble on pickles with his sister still talking as she trailed him.

Sarah looked out of place and abandoned in the kitchen with Laura.

"Can you stir the gravy for me?" Laura asked, hoping to relax Sarah by giving her something to do. "Don't mind Karen, she's like a mother hen with her little brother."

Sarah giggled politely.

"Where are you from?" Laura asked, sneaking looks at Sarah. She had seen black people in TV and occasionally in the grocery store, but never in her own house. Sarah looked exotic in the sanctity of the kitchen.

"Detroit. Or really Lansing, now."

"You have family in Detroit?" Laura asked and then wondered if she assumed that because of her dark skin.

"No, not really, I guess," Sarah said into the steam rising from the gravy. "I grew up in foster care."

"You don't have any family? You poor thing," Laura said and immediately felt like she was being condescending with her comments. "Well, how was your ride up here?"

"Oh, pretty good," Sarah offered, meeting Laura's eyes. "I've never been this far north."

"Things go a lot farther north than this. Karen brought her family from near the bridge."

"What did you say about me?" Karen walked back into the kitchen.

"I was telling Sarah that you live up by the bridge," Laura said. "Where's Sam?"

"He's watching the game."

"You're going to have to fend for yourself around here," Laura joked to Sarah.

"Hmp. Sam's last wife got so scared, she ran off." Karen mumbled with a mouthful of pickle. "We didn't like her."

Laura eyed her daughter. She was beginning to feel nervous about what Karen might be thinking about Sarah. Peter had yet to lay eyes on this pretty little girl that Sam had neglected to say was black. African-American for those who were politically correct. Nigger in Peter's eyes. Laura cringed. She hoped Sam had neglected to identify this girl's race because she had raised him right.

"Oh, I wouldn't worry too much, Sarah. Sam has only had good things to say about you," Laura said while spooning fluffy mounds of potato into a serving bowl. "Karen. Can you tell the men that it's time to eat?"

"Her bark is worse than her bite," Laura informed Sarah and handed her the heavy bowl. "Here, go put this on the table."

Laura scurried around the kitchen and carried out the platter of roast chicken as Peter came into the dining room and saw Sarah for the first time. Laura watched him carefully as he stared at the girl while he took his seat.

"Dad, this is Sarah," Sam said, as he pulled out a chair for her to sit in.

"I figured as much," he replied, finally breaking his gaze.

Laura sat quickly between her husband and Sarah and grabbed at her hand. "Say grace, Peter," she instructed him. Sam, Karen, Mike and the boys all joined hands and bowed their heads as the patriarch blessed the food. Laura did not hear his words as she fervently made her own prayers that Peter would not insult Sarah.

"Amen," Laura joined her family. Everyone was polite to Sarah throughout the meal but Laura still felt apprehensive.

During dessert, Sam made the announcement that he and Sarah were engaged. Everyone congratulated them.

"Are you going to have the wedding in the spring?" Karen directed the question at Sam.

"We're going to do it on New Year's Day," Sarah happily divulged.

"What? This coming New Year's Day?" Karen voiced concern. "Oh, that's much too soon to plan a wedding. You should have sent invitations out already if you're going to do that."

"It's not a big deal," Sam sounded edgy. "It's going to be small with just family and a few friends."

"Not a big deal," Karen pestered. "Come on, where are you going to get a hall and what church is going to hold a wedding after all the Christmas hoopla?"

"We were hoping to do it here," Sarah looked hesitantly at Laura. "If that's okay with you. It was Sam's idea."

"I think that's a great idea," Laura heard herself say exuberantly, then she looked at her husband sitting with his hands clasped, dessert in front of him untouched. "Is that okay Peter?"

"Dunno. I just think marriage vows should be done in the sanctity of a church. Can they find a minister who will marry them outside the church?"

Sarah looked at Sam as if waiting for him to answer. "We have a friend who we want to perform the ceremony."

"Oh, you've got to be kidding," Karen slammed her fist on the table. "Of all the pagan things you could do. Is he a ship captain or something?"

"It's my marriage, not yours," he glared at Karen

"Well, look what happened to your first."

"You're never going to drop it, are you."

"I'm just looking out for you," Karen said condescendingly.

"Karen," Mike tugged at his wife's sleeve.

"Do you wonder why I didn't introduce Sarah to you sooner?"

Laura held her breath. A leading question, if there ever was one. Laura feared what the answer might be.

"Sam," Sarah said with a force of power behind her voice. "Stop. It's not worth it. You're getting upset about nothing."

Laura watched the fire diffuse in her son in a way she had never seen before. He and Karen regularly got into arguments, but it usually ended with Sam storming off. He sat in his chair and mellowed back into ease with his future wife's hand holding his.

No doubt, Sarah was going to be good for her son, Laura thought. Selfishly she wanted to believe this girl would be good for her too. Unfortunately, she knew loving Sarah would not absolve her of her own passive complicity.

"How did you and Sam meet?" Mike asked.

"A roommate from college introduced us," Sam replied.

"Is he black too?" Karen asked.

Laura was intrigued and proud of Sam's acceptance of diversity. She wanted to know how they met, too, but noticed Sarah look away after Karen asked the question. How was that question not appropriate, Laura thought, feeling obtuse.

"No. Why would you think that?" Sam taunted Karen.

"I just," Karen stumbled. "I just figured..."

"Because Sarah's black?"

Laura watched Karen glare at Sam. Mike looked at Karen and the boys looked at Sarah while Peter stared into his plate.

"I've had black friends before. I'm not insensitive. I don't see color. I just see people's worth. Anyhow, Sarah doesn't even sound black," Karen argued.

"Peter, eat your pie," Laura pushed the dish closer to him. "I made it the way you like it."

Karen used her father for a diversion too. "You're awful quiet, Dad. Everything okay?"

"Hmph. I don't have any opinion's."

Laura held her breath. Oh, he had opinions, all right. She felt the knot in her stomach return from when she had taken food and given Karen's shoes to the little black girl living in the hovel, so long ago. She knew she needed to do something, but did not know what to do. Giving Karen's shoes away had been the wrong thing. That little girl had no doubt felt ashamed by Laura's actions.

"Blacks have just as much chance to be successful as anyone else these days," Laura tried and knew it was wrong as she looked into Sarah's eyes.

"Do you eat greens?" one of Karen's boys asked Sarah.

"Yep," she said, a big smile attempted to mask her ridged shoulders. "And I like lima beans too."

"Gross," the boys said in chorus and stuck their tongues out at Sarah, laughing.

Karen seemed uncomfortable with the acceptance between her boys and Sarah. "Dad, one of your favorite sayings is birds of a feather flock together. You and I think alike. Some people have to stick together while other's need to stay away. The biggest hurt a person can inflict on themselves is not knowing their place." With no response from him, she bullied him. "A wolf in sheep's clothing does not make him a sheep."

Laura, feeling a growing disconnect from her family sitting around the table, interjected. "You need to stop arguing like you're wolves protecting your territory. We're not birds either," she glared at Karen and then turned to Sarah to clarify her meaning. "We're just human beings. All of us."

All of it had occurred so long ago. Yet the memories seemed to unfold in front of her eyes like they had just happened. The flames licked at the last bits of fabric and papers. Laura stood at the side of the fire pit and enjoyed the smell of the bonfire after she finished burning the other boxes of papers. Smokey and sooty but also sweet smelling as the wood released its intimate scent. The fire beckoning it out, dancing with it, creating a heady and lustful scent. The mix of elements working together. Fire, wood, air. If one was missing, it would not work. She knew Sam and Sarah would be at the house soon. The fire was almost out and she was about to leave when she heard fallen branches crunching under footsteps behind her. Startled, she turned and saw Sam and Sarah.

"Hey Mom," Sam said with concern in his voice. "What are you doing?"

"Cleaning out some of your father's things," she said as a matter of fact. "Don't worry, I have boxes in the house for you to take home. Karen too."

Laura noticed Sam looking into the fire pit, trying to discover what she would never let him know. She ignored him and grabbed Sarah's hands.

"How are you dear?" she asked Sarah.

"I'm okay."

"Let's go to the house. You two have to be starved. I didn't realize I was out here so long." Laura looped her arm around Sarah's, guiding her towards the house. "You can help me in the kitchen."

Sam stayed a moment longer, observing the fire pit. Laura knew there was nothing but a log, charred to coals and lots of grey white ashes. What had been there a short time ago was now irrelevant. It was gone.

CHAPTER 7

Laura was so weak that all she could do was open her eyes in response to the night nurse. She watched the nurse drop three pills into a small canister. They plinked against the plastic bottom. With a few twists of the nurse's wrist she dumped the pills, now a powder, into a small cup of applesauce and fed Laura a few spoonfuls.

"I'm so tired," Laura whispered.

"That's okay Laura. I won't bother you until morning. Have a good night," The nurse said and clicked off the overhead light.

Laura's eyes were still open in the dark when the nurse left. The light from the hall spilled into the room, highlighting the other bed that was made up perfectly smooth. A few days before, Laura's roommate had been wheeled out, covered up from head to toe. The next day her family came and took all of her belongings with them. Laura vaguely remembered the few quiet tears that were shed while they boxed her things up. She closed her eyes, not wanting to watch uninvited.

"I'm so tired," Laura whispered into the room. She finally felt herself drifting off to sleep when her hand was picked up by someone else's hands.

"It's okay Laura. It's Mother," The voice said in soothing way.

Laura felt comforted and didn't bother to open her eyes. Despite all those years of her mother's aloof affections, she was finding solace with these bedside visits. Without explanation of her mother's uncharacteristic tenderness, Laura was not ready to absolve her quite yet and felt she deserved to know her motives. She kept her other feelings of jealousy, confusion and inadequacy at bay. They were the least likely of emotions she would have anticipated to present themselves with eternity stretched out in front of her.

"I'm excited to see what it's like," Laura said and pushed confronting her mother out of her mind. Within this dreamy state of being coddled by her mother, there was a distinct reality that her mother could return to the cold emotions Laura hated. It was not worth confronting her now, maybe when she was not so tired. "I want to see Little Andrew and Harry again. You and Father. Grandmother and Grandfather. But I'm scared too."

"Everyone is scared of it Laura. Some more than others. Some are so scared of dying that it consumes a person and they forget what living is," Martha stroked Laura's forehead. "Go to sleep

Laura. If you're ready to go, I'm here. I will stay with you."

"Is it true, Mother?" Laura spoke after a few moments. "Is there life after death?"

"It isn't life, Laura, it's death. But it isn't the end of everything that we have been led to believe."

Moving into the nursing home had such finality that it was the end of her life. Her beauty had faded behind the white hair that adamantly tried to stop the void of color, but a pale yellow was all it could muster. The wrinkles lay across her face and hands like crumpled tissue paper that someone tried to smooth out, but the telltale creases refused to negate its existence. She had come to the end with nothing more to accomplish. With death looming so close in the future, Laura was unable to find something to hope for or look forward to in the confines of her institutional home.

But with the dead remembering her, there was nothing to force the members of her family, still living, to remember her. If her possessions slowly became detached from memories of her, little by little, she knew she would die in their memories too. It would happen, she had done it herself. She remembered how her memory changed over time after Harry died. Her parents. Her last baby. Peter. It was different with Little Andrew because she had been so young. But for a month or two after the deaths, every waking thought was consumed by the loss. Her dreams were filled with animated interactions. After a while, the intensity subsided to a couple of times a day, to once a day, and then to occasionally when something would trigger a memory. A sip of cool water might make her think how her loved one would never experience that again. But now, she was the one dying. The one who would be forgotten, little by little, piece by piece, until she no longer existed.

Laura relaxed and her breathing became even and calm. Her mother continued holding her hand. About to be released from life, she was still afraid of being forgotten, like her own fleeting memories that refused to retrieve the question Sarah had asked so many months before. She did not have to be afraid of being alone anymore, just forgotten.

CHAPTER 8

Under a gray winter sky, Rose made her way along the edge of the forest. Snow sat on the leafless limbs of the trees, highlighting the graceful outlines that the sun would not. The whiteness of the snow created a starkness, exaggerating the solid gray of the trunks that moved upwards towards the sky. In the distance, the vertical figures of the trees almost turned to black. The ephemeral existence of tender green leaves only a memory as the stark contrasts dominated the beauty of the season.

To her left, snow covered the tired field of broken corn stalks. In the blazing sun of summer they had reached so high, waving their silky brown tassels. Now they were bent over with brittle leaves rustling sadly when the wind blew across the field. Snow was beginning to fall and her long skirt swept the snow behind her. From under a dark woolen bonnet, her face peeked out with rosy cheeks and her breath came out in frosty puffs. She drew her dark grey cloak around her and tightly grasped it in front of her, bracing against the wind.

Turning, she entered the pine forest between two towering Ironwood trees marking a path overgrown with brush, all but erased by Mother Nature. It looked neglected and untraveled but she knew this way well, still clear in her mind. It was the path to her family.

Rose fondly remembered the winters when the trees glistened under the hoar frost. The branches would hang low, under the heavy condensation. It would stay that way until the sun melted the eerie and quiet fogginess blanketing the earth.

The silence of the outdoors would be broken by children's laughter and shrieks of delight. Frosty puffs of breath would come magically out of the children's noses and mouths. The snow would crunch under their feet. The snowy forest enchanted the imagination into taking them to the Swiss Alps or the polar caps.

Rose would call out to her children playing at the edge of the forest that surrounded their home. "Laura, Harry, Little Andrew," she would holler into the wilderness. "Dinner time." An echo from the woods would repeat her announcement.

She felt pride for her boys, her first born, Harry and Little Andrew, the baby. It did not matter how big they grew, her maternal instinct locked its arms around them, refusing to let go. But there was an importance with sons, they carried the family name to the next generation, allowing the family name to live on.

Laura, by nature of being the only girl, should have been spoiled with affections. Despite Laura's sunny disposition, Rose did not know how to nurture this daughter who should be a reflection of herself, her own flesh and blood. Rose did not see herself in Laura's little face, like she did with Harry and Little Andrew. She saw her beautiful sister, Lily, never admitting it was jealousy she felt towards her. She saw her mother, Julia, a stately woman of refinement who had been deposited in the northern wilds of Michigan. Rose felt her mother's contempt for her, figuring it was her own fault for not being pretty. She felt inferior living in the shadows of her mother and sister.

Those big green eyes of her daughter, like upside down smiles when she laughed, reminded Rose of the females she could not even compete with. She felt it was important that Laura did not grow up to think her beauty should keep her from knowing hard work. It would be what was in her heart that would matter. Rose was determined to not let Laura grow up believing her beauty entitled her to anything. But how to nurture a child she feared, she did not know. When she forced herself to be affectionate towards Laura, it felt uncomfortable, like embracing a stranger. Harry and Little Andrew always fit in the crook of her own body whenever she drew them close with a one armed hug.

Rose pushed a lock of stray grey hair out of her eyes. Her hair had turned when she was thirty-two. The same year Little Andrew drowned and grief saturated her heart until it burst into tiny pieces. Her body became a dry and brittle husk to a spirit that left her insides empty and hollow as she existed from one day to the next. If God was teaching her a lesson, she did not know what it was. Then Harry died. It did not make sense. It was not even grief she felt. Whatever the feeling was, it insulated her from feeling alive, from feeling like she had any reasons left for any joy. It was not the deaths, but all of the years and events that reminded her of what she did not have, what she had lost, like watching other people's children grow when her own Little Andrew would not. Sometimes she imagined the wind carried her baby's voice calling for her.

Becoming a parent should have been an opportunity for Rose to vindicate her own tragic relationship with her own mother, but she was still unable to be a mother to Laura and knew her daughter resented it. But life was not as difficult for her daughter as it was for herself. Now, in the ironies of death, she was working on becoming the mother to Laura that she had never been. Her daughter's forgiveness might not fix the damage between them, or she might not even grant her forgiveness. But Rose wanted a chance to explain her own shortcomings, hoping to find peace with her only daughter. It would be up to Laura to accept what she had to offer. Rose trudged along the path, musing about how little she knew back then. She missed her daughter. She could not wait until Laura could join them.

All three of her children would be with her again and Rose held her excitement like a wrapped gift, not knowing what was concealed beneath, but so sure of the pleasure she would find when it was revealed. She finally realized it was her precious children who gave her a place in the world. It was as if they were her second chance at existing in the world as their mother, no longer needing to be known as Lily's plain sister or the wife of James who preferred other women's beds. Guiding Laura from life into death would be her gift to her daughter. Her boys had greeted her at her own arrival, when for so long, Rose had been sure she would never see them again.

In the clearing of Jack Pine was the home where she and her husband, James, one by one, conceived their three children. It was a chance meeting between Rose and James. Rose had gotten a job working at the general store. Her mother was indifferent about her working in town and seemed to not care that a reputation might grow from her daughter waiting on lumberjacks. Rose's father, Levi, tried to shield her from her mother's viciousness, but it was usually ineffective as he was preoccupied in placating his wife, Julia. For Rose, she was happy for the money and the chance to get away from the house. Her mother's dreams of Lily having many suitors and picking the wealthiest and the most socially prominent died with their pretty daughter. Rose wanted to prove to her mother she could find a husband too when her mother lamented that it had been her pretty daughter who had died. Rose was really not so plain, but anyone held in comparison with her mother or sister would be considered dull.

It was late fall when James and his cousin traveled from Ontario to northern Michigan to lumberjack. In eastern Canada lumbering had slowed down but in northern Michigan it was in full swing. Some of the men from the camps would come into the store and be boisterous and joke with each other. Any woman within a half mile of them was subject to their flirting or harassment, depending on the receiver's feelings about it. Rose had become aware of the one group who frequented the store. One of the men was a head shorter than the rest and always seemed to be surrounded by the taller men as they cajoled and made jokes about him, calling him 'Shorty.' Rose flushed in embarrassment for him when he was pushed up to the counter where she stood.

"Go ahead, ask her," she heard the men encouraging him.

He stood silently at the counter and looked at his balled up hands he laid on the counter edge. "Better be careful with her," another comment from the group came. "A scar like that, I'd hate to see the loser of that fight."

Rose's face was unable to deepen any further in color at the shame of the scar across her nose and cheek. He looked up and looked reproachfully at her, as if it would apologize for his friend's crassness.

"What's your name," he said quietly. The men drifted away and roamed the length of the store.

"Rose," she said, noticing he was a bit shorter than she.

"I'm James."

"What can I help you with?" Rose asked, working on grasping all of her composure. The girls that were not considered good, would flirt back with the men. She reassured herself she was good even though she delighted in the attention.

"The circus is coming to town next week. Would you like to go?"

Looking back, Rose did not remember saying yes, but she must have because she went with him and saw the tiger show and the acrobats and the horses doing tricks. He continued courting her and on the sixth visit they had together he kissed her. Rose felt so pretty with him kissing her. She dared to imagine he could make her feel beautiful.

"Stop, James," Rose said after a few minutes and pushed him away.

"I don't think you want me to," he said and rubbed his mustache on the nape of her neck.

"I'm not that kind of girl," she pushed him away again.

"What kind of girl is that?" he grabbed her close so her chest slammed into his. "Married girls do this."

"I'm not married."

"Maybe I should marry you then," he leaned forward to try and kissed her.

"Maybe, or you will?" Rose asked, knowing her chance had come, but wanted to be sure.

"I'll marry you," he said moving his hands along the buttons of her dress.

She was ecstatic that he wanted to marry her, even despite the humiliation she felt after pulling her skirt back down. She was wanted, she could be loved, *'not just Lily,'* she wanted to shout at her mother, but only said "James and I are getting married."

After Laura, Harry and Little Andrew were born, Rose did her best to make her home welcoming and continued to forgive James every time he slept in another woman's bed. Now, all that was left of the original house was the clearing.

"Mother's back," Little Andrew announced to Harry and Grandfather Levi. He held a stick in his hand frozen in mid air when he spoke. He had been knocking snow off of tree boughs with his stick when his mother had appeared.

"Did you see Laura?" Little Andrew followed his mother.

"Let your mother sit down," Grandfather Levi bellowed with the pipe still clenched between his teeth. His long white beard insulated his face from all except the most bitter winds. Under his nose and the corners of his mouth his whiskers were yellowed from pipe smoke. The whites of his eyes were the color of old parchment down to the swirly script when handwriting was an art form. The furrow on his brow had softened at his daughter's return.

Rose sat down on a fallen log and smoothed out her long skirt. The dark navy dress with light pinstripes was utilitarian in style and the fading from wear added to her matronly look. Harry sat down next to her. His cap was slightly crooked on his head and he wore a red flannel Mackinac jacket, always fashionable in this chilly climate.

Rose sighed. "Well, I saw her," she paused, making sure she had everyone's attention. "She knew who I was."

They seemed to hold their breath for a second.

"She knew you?" Harry exclaimed.

"What does that mean?" Little Andrew asked. His memory of his sister, Laura, was fleeting.

"She's going to be with us soon."

There was quiet except for the wind blowing through the pine needles.

Grandfather Levi took his pipe in his hand and rubbed his chin thoughtfully. "Is she suffering Rose? Is she suffering?" he begged to know.

"Not really, she's just waiting to be with her family."

A bough up in the treetops squeaked.

"Sam's wife, Sarah, was visiting her," Rose offered.

"The colored girl?" Grandfather Levi asked.

"Yes, that's the one." Rose shifted her weight to a more comfortable position.

"Times have changed," Grandfather Levi considered. "I guess color doesn't matter anymore."

"This girl is different," Rose stated. "Laura's lucky to have someone like her."

"How is Laura?" Little Andrew begged his mother. "It's been so long since we've seen her."

"Laura gets real confused with what is going on now," Rose said, to which Grandfather Levi shook his head sadly. "But this girl, Sarah, she doesn't push her. She's real gentle with her. Laura likes her. She'll sit there for the longest time and just hold her hand." Rose seemed satisfied with that.

Grandfather Levi seemed lost in thought. Harry and Little Andrew stayed quiet, hoping their mother would continue.

"The only one who's missing is Laura," Grandfather Levi said, looking at Rose with her two sons.

"How much longer 'till she's with us?" Little Andrew asked.

"She's ready. She's just waiting for her body to let go."

"Any other news about her family?"

"Sarah's looking for Julia," Rose eyed her father. "She's having a hard time finding her."

"How can we help her find Grandmother Julia?" Little Andrew asked.

"Really aren't suppose to," Harry said.

"It's a shame. For so long Julia has been forgotten," Grandfather Levi said wistfully about his long lost wife. "This Sarah wants everyone in our family to be remembered."

"Yes, she's wonderful. But it is a baby that she would really love," Rose said. "She understands what family means. She thinks she can be connected to our family if she finds all the lost connections."

"Do you think that she's going to have a baby to add to our family?" Little Andrew asked.

"We really won't know until it happens," Harry said.

"She's family already." Grandfather Levi half scolded. "Don't need no baby to be in our family."

An owl hooted in the distance, distracting their attention. The conversation hushed and they gazed up at the stars, still twinkling against the strength of the bright full moon rising. Rose envisioned her beautiful little girl with brown bobbing curls at her side once again. Harry and Little Andrew trailing behind, just like old times, but better.

"I'm going to let James know that Laura is coming," Rose said. "I'd like to return to Laura soon. I promised her that she wouldn't be alone."

"Can I go with you to see Father?" Little Andrew asked, tugging at Rose's sleeve.

"No Andrew, I need you to stay here with your Grandfather Levi."

"But Ma..."

"Andrew," Grandfather Levi spoke sternly. "Listen to your mother."

"You'll be okay without me for a couple of days, won't you Father?" Rose asked.

"We'll make do. Laura is going to need everyone around her when she comes. We'll keep busy and spread the word while you're gone."

The snow had stopped falling, creating a stillness, blanketing the dancing leaves of the autumn season. Up above, the treetops swayed, softly whispering their memories of when Laura used to run underneath their shade. It was the season of rest and with each new generation, the season of rebirth would not be forgotten. She was coming back home. Laura would be with them again.

CHAPTER 9

Sarah untied the ribbon around a box wrapped in brightly colored wrapping paper.

"Happy birthday, honey," Sam told her as he shoved his hands into his jean pockets and leaned against the Formica counter. He had taken a break from stirring the pot of spaghetti sauce he had been laboring over all afternoon and presented Sarah with a gift. "I was going to give it to you at dinner, but I couldn't wait."

She took the paper off, smiling in anticipation of what surprise awaited her, while her dark curls danced around her face.

Inside the pale pink velvet box was a single pearl suspended from a gold chain.

"It's so pretty. Thank you," she said and embraced him. "Help me put it on, will you?"

She turned and held the curls at the nape of her neck so he could clasp the necklace. "What do you think?" she asked as she turned around.

"It looks beautiful. You look beautiful."

"And you need to change your clothes," she teased him. "Your sister and her husband are going to be here any time."

It was the weekend, which meant sweatshirts for Sam. He proudly wore his kelly green Michigan State University sweatshirt which looked like it had more than served its purpose. A tee shirt, utilitarian in effort to keep him warm, peaked out from under the sweatshirt collar.

"I don't have to get dressed up. It's not my birthday, it's yours."

Sarah fingered the smoothness of the pearl hanging from the fine gold necklace.

"You probably want earrings to go with that, or do you have some other wish?" he asked.

Her smile faded and she started gathering up the wrapping paper.

"What have I wanted for the last few years?" she said quietly, refusing to look at him. She had always requested very little of him and now that she had voiced her want, she felt guilty.

Sam sighed and shrugged his shoulders.

She played with a tendril of ribbon between her fingers, pulling it taut and watching it coil back on itself when she let go. "I have a physical this week," Sarah started. "I would like to ask for a referral to a fertility specialist."

"I guess that would be a good idea," Sam said.

"I want to know if this is something you're willing to pursue with me."

"I don't understand what you're saying. I've told you I'm ready for kids." Sam's hazel eyes concentrated on Sarah.

"I know that. I mean, if we're referred to a specialist, you may have to undergo tests also. Are you willing to do that?"

"Go ahead. I know this means a lot to you. I kind of think it would be cool to have a son."

"Or a daughter," Sarah laughed nervously at Sam's omission. She could feel the laugh echo off her insides as if they were empty and the hope of having children was fading fast. The possibility of not having a baby was now a reality. They had spoken it out loud. Before, the conversations had revolved around how they looked forward to children and the noise and clutter filling up their lives. Imagining these dreams solid as a vapor, she looked down at her hands, knowing if she reached out, her hands would surround nothing, folding in on themselves, making fists and only feeling the cold mist settling on her skin, something that was real but could not be hers.

Sarah wished Sam's mother was not losing her grip on life at such a fast pace in the nursing home. Laura was the closest thing to a mother Sarah ever had. She would have understood, at least the part involving her obsession of wanting to know herself through her own child, her own flesh and blood. Other women had the same dilemma, but she was at a loss of understanding how they coped. Laura would have known the right words to say,

Sarah was sure, as she groped around, trying to make sense of her feelings.

But there were other reasons she kept to herself. It was important to hide those other motives that Sam or Laura would not understand and perhaps find her a fraud if they knew how vigilantly she wanted to belong to a family. She insatiably craved to be a part of something that would nurture her, accept her and tell her that she belonged, she was wanted and was someone that others could depend on. With Sam and his family she could do this, but only if she acted white enough.

Raised in foster care, she spent many years with her white family whose ingrained beliefs were repeated like mantra, *'if you act white, if you talk white, you might get ahead.'* There was no denying this as fact for Sarah. Over and over she saw how people feared color, that the lighter a black person, the less scary and threatening they were. She knew the white person's saunter in the grocery store and how it quickened with suspicion when they noticed or realized she was near them. She knew the sound of car door locks being engaged in the parking lot or at a stoplight when a black person appeared.

There was no denying that black babies were the cutest little things with their big soft brown eyes and creamy whites of their eyes contrasting with the darkness of their skin. Even as young girls, there is an innocence bound within stiffness of their pigtails. But the larger they grow, the more threatening they must become as Sarah was moved to a black foster care family. But with the black families, she was told, "You are so stuck up. You act like you're white, thinking you're better than us. Those white families got you thinking you're white."

Still, it was the white people who had the good jobs and the important jobs. You did not see reporters or government officials talking street talk or walking around with a pick stuck in half a do or wearing do-rags in public. What white people had was very enticing. The well off black families did not have any less than the white families, except the white families got more respect. Sarah knew the blacks would see her as a sell out, but given the choice, when neither black nor white accepted her, she was determined to assimilate with those who got more.

She could be anything and anybody she wanted to be, as the State had long ago exhausted their attempts in finding any relatives who could provide care for her. The idea should have been liberating, but she was condemned to be alone in life and not know anyone she had a blood connection with. Sarah knew she had not been alone at her birth, but that was the last time she had been intimately connected to someone, her mother. For so long she did not dare to believe she could belong to a family.

Then she met Sam. There was something about his personality that allowed her to relax the gnawing fear of being alone. She smiled, thinking about her husband trying to get her to laugh, as she attempted to suppress giggles that would escape into a belly laugh. His horrible imitation of women singers would always elicit a laugh from her. Sam would also make her lose her composure when he told her a joke and messed up the punch line or forgot it completely.

To her delight, Sam introduced Sarah to the family as his fiancée. She had been apprehensive going north with him to meet them the first time. She was afraid of her skin that looked kissed by the sun, even in the dead of winter, standing out in a sea of white, might forever exclude her.

Sam's father, Peter, was quiet and not very outgoing and died shortly after Sam and Sarah married. Laura had embraced Sarah with great welcome. She knew Sam was pleased, while his sister, Karen, was jealous of the budding relationship. Sarah tried to stay undaunted by Karen's critical tongue. With little imagination she could hear Karen's voice rattle through her head.

"Mom," Karen shook her head. "You've already told Sarah that story. God only knows how many times I've had to hear it."

"I'm sorry if I tell the same stories over and over," Laura apologized to Sarah. "I'm prone to repeating myself, but I don't want Sam and Karen to forget them."

"I don't mind. Someday I hope those stories will be mine too." Sarah face reddened, embarrassed by her own boldness.

"Oh, honey," Laura reassured her. "I'm completely flattered and with the wedding coming up, you're already part of the family."

Belonging was a gift she cherished by having a husband to celebrate her birthday with. There was pride of ownership in calling him 'my husband' or hearing him say 'my wife.' But there were different levels of being alone on the journey through life. Sam's love was not the answer to all of them.

The doorbell rang, breaking the silence that had overtaken their conversation.

"I'll get it," Sarah said.

Karen and Mike appeared as Sarah opened the door.

"Come in," Sarah said excitedly. "Come in."

"Happy Birthday, Sarah!" Mike exclaimed as he gave her a big hug.

"Sam's in the kitchen," Sarah led them down the hall into the bright white kitchen. Glimpses of whiteness in the other rooms could be seen on the way. White walls, white furniture; this was definitely a house not broken in yet by children.

"I see you dressed for the occasion," Karen said sarcastically as she held Sam at a distance when he tried to hug her.

"I like my sweatshirt."

"It's a rag," Karen complained. "You're ex-wife would have never let you wear that."

Sarah stiffened at the cloaked insult. It was a wonder that they were as close as they were when it was Karen's mission to make Sam conform.

"Why do you have to constantly remind me of her?" Sam responded with irritation. "That's the whole reason I divorced her, to get away from her."

"Well," Karen cocked an eyebrow at no one in particular.

"Drop it Sam," Sarah cut in. "You're stuck with me now."

"What are you cooking, little brother?" Mike asked with enthusiastic gaiety. "It smells great."

"Spaghetti sauce to beat all other sauces," Sam gloated and returned to stirring the pot. Some of the ingredients had obviously made their way to the front of Sam's sweatshirt. The humidity in the kitchen had coaxed out the curl in his brown hair. The combination made him look a little more like a mad scientist making dinner. "It's an old family secret recipe," he divulged.

Sarah smirked at Mike as Karen asked why she didn't know about it and that he should tell her.

"The secret ingredient is to add a little bit of Italian," Sam said as he proceeded to stick his finger into the sauce and then into his mouth, dramatically slurping the red juice.

"You're as Italian as the Eiffel Tower," Karen said, unamused.

"Yes," Sarah agreed. "Considering that your family most likely came from Ireland."

"How are you coming on the genealogy?" Mike asked Sarah.

"I've hit a road block. I'm looking for Julia, but there are several of them and I can't get the lineage to match this woman that was Laura's grandmother. There's one listed as marrying a Levi Heywood. The first name is right, but until I can determine the correct last name I don't want to falsely document a link. Laura has it written down as Levi Harwood." Sarah continued shaking her head back and forth, thinking about the inconsistencies. "The family histories that flow down each family isn't exactly the same in detail when you merge them with other people's genealogy work."

"How are you going to figure this guy out?" Mike asked, thoroughly impressed.

"Oh, I have an email to the person who has this information."

"How are you finding this information?" he wanted to know.

"So far I've mostly found leads on the internet. The Mormons have a pretty good web site. Other sites are very commercial and hold info hostage until you pay up the fees they request.

"Speaking of Mormons," Karen said impatiently. "What did you do with that bottle of wine, Mike?"

"Pasta's going to be ready in about five minutes," Sam said as he pointed Mike to a drawer that held the corkscrew.

"I hope you don't mind eating in here," Sarah said getting wineglasses out of the cupboard. "I have the genealogy stuff all over the dining room table."

"It's funny that you spend so much time researching our family," Karen said to Sarah.

"I don't know why," Sarah said, trying to ignore Karen's observation that this was not Sarah's family by birthright. "The more connections I find, the more connected I feel." She tried to use her comments to hide the hurt feelings that surfaced. She remembered Karen forbidding her to ask Laura to move in with her and Sam. She daydreamed of Karen going into her and Sam's bedroom and discovering the silver plate hair brush on the dressing table. "Your mother wanted me to have it," Sarah would tell her and imagined watching Karen's face flush with anger or maybe even jealousy. Sarah knew it was mean to even think this. Who was Karen to determine who her mother decided to love? Sarah felt if Laura wanted to love her, she would accept it.

"You are family," Mike said. "I think it's great that you're doing it."

"I've told my kids a hundred times, stories about the family, but I don't know how much they listen," Karen said. "It's like when I was young, I was told all kinds of stories, but now that they are important for me to remember, the storytellers can't tell them anymore."

"I wish I had asked Mom more things," Sam said stirring the pot of pasta. "Do you recall Mom and Dad fighting whenever he came home late?" he asked Karen.

"Vaguely," she answered.

"I never figured out what they were arguing about. I don't thinking it was alcohol. He used to come in and kiss me goodnight thinking I was still asleep and I couldn't smell anything on his breath. I remember him drinking at other times and he had this odd sweet smell on his breath when he did."

"Well, I doubt that he was having an affair. Mom wouldn't have stood for it." Karen stated as a matter of fact.

"Do you remember," Sam started again. "A couple of weeks after Dad died, we went to her house?"

"Yes."

"Sarah and I got there early. Mom was out at the bonfire burning some of Dad's things. I thought she acted kind of odd."

"What did she say?" Karen wanted to know, her interest now piqued.

"She kind of blew it off. I can't imagine what she was burning."

"Strange," was Karen's reply. "Do you remember the time Mom gave my shoes away?"

This was a story Sarah had not heard and she perked her ears and heard Sam respond with an uncharacteristic sullen affected "vaguely." Karen became animated and directed herself towards Sarah, who had shown interest.

"We were just kids. She took us out to this place, squalor like you've never seen. The little black girl didn't have shoes and Mom made me take mine off and give them to her. They were my favorite shoes. Oh, how she fought with me. I thought she was going to beat me," Karen chuckled. "It was so out of character for her. Mom has always been the most kind and gentle person I've ever known. I guess it was silly to be so attached to a pair of shoes. But that made me mad. It's the only time I ever saw her so vicious."

An embarrassed blaze fell on Sarah's face. She wondered if Karen saw her as some hillbilly sharecropper. Inner city ghetto maybe, but still it was insulting the way Karen disdained the whole event. Sarah heard the negative relating to the little girl's skin tone.

"Did she say why she did it?" Mike asked.

"No. She just said 'we take care of our own'."

"Who were these people?" Sarah ventured into the conversation carefully.

"Supposedly they're descendants of slaves who were brought here," Sam claimed.

"Hmm. Imagine that," Karen said.

Sarah looked up to see Karen staring at her with wonderment and then looked away. If she only acted white enough, Sam's sister might quit seeing her only as black, trying to discount her at every turn. She knew Laura consciously saw her as black too, but tried to compensate with overabundant acceptance as if she was begging for forgiveness, which made Sarah feel guilty. But forgiveness and love were two different things. She loved Laura regardless and wanted to be part of Laura's family forever. A baby would be Sarah's legitimate claim to

Sam's family and all the history and all the memories.

"Sarah was able to get a lot of stories from Mom in the past few months," Sam said, apparently finished with Karen's story. The reference to Sarah inadvertently irritated Karen, but Sarah caught on and rebuked his claim.

"She hasn't always been clear or cooperative, but I guess I have a lot of patience with her after working with the kind of children that I do in therapy," Sarah said gently to Karen. "Anyway, she isn't mean or rude to me like some of the kids at work are."

"That's kids for you, today," Karen said. "Too spoiled and no respect."

"I've had some of those too," Sarah said setting forks next to the plates that she had put out earlier. "But many times some of these children with traumatic brain injuries are frightened and don't understand what has happened to them. If there's injury or change of the chemical pathways, some of the nicest kids can become some of the worst."

"Do they ever recover?" Mike asked.

"Sometimes, but not always fully. There was one little girl that was just a terror and delighted in targeting me with her poor behavior. Before she finished her therapy she came to me and apologized with a big hug." Tears hung in Sarah's lower lids. "That's the reason I keep going back to work."

"But your mother," Sarah continued. "She isn't going to recover." Teary eyes switched to Karen. Mike, more intrigued with what Sarah was saying, didn't notice.

"Are there similarities between brain injury and Alzheimer's?" He asked.

"I'm not saying she has Alzheimer's. I dare say she has dementia. I guess some patients have a marked personality change. Usually for the worse, but in rare cases some of the worst personalities become docile and gentle. I don't know as much about that as I do with traumatic brain injury."

"It's really hard to let go," Karen said wiping her eyes with the napkin from the place setting where she sat. Mike had finally tuned into his wife's emotions and he proceeded to rub her shoulders.

"I know what you mean," Sam said. "Mom will always be my mom. I go to her when I need her, but I'm afraid that's changing very fast."

"I just feel like I'm not doing enough for her," Karen blubbered. "Do you remember Kitty Parsons? She and her mother never got along and she ended up taking care of her at home for four years. You know what she said to me afterwards? She was broke and tired. She felt bad that she didn't do more and she didn't even love her mother. I love my mother and I feel just as inadequate."

Sarah pushed Sam towards the table and took over finishing the pasta.

"I keep telling Karen that her mother isn't suffering," Mike said to Sam and Sarah, but more as a reaffirmation to Karen. "If her mother doesn't need anything and she is loved, that is enough."

Sarah set the hot pasta in the middle of the table and slid into the seat next to Karen.

"I don't want to forget these different things about her when she dies," Karen said and dried her eyes with a new napkin Sarah had slipped her.

"Look at your hands," Sarah beckoned, picking up Karen's hand. "They look like hers, don't they?"

"No, these are my fathers. They look just like my fathers." Karen let go of Sarah's and held them up for display. Sarah put her own in her lap and looked down.

"I'm sorry, Sarah," Karen said earnestly. "This is your birthday. It's supposed to be happy for you."

"Don't worry, it is happy for me. I'm with family," She affirmed and squeezed Karen's hand, trying to believe she could forgive this woman who seemed to want to protect her family from an interloper with different colored skin.

CHAPTER 10

Heavy calligraphy filled framed documents above the doctor's head, as if the answers were contained in the frilly loops of academia. Sarah concentrated on reading word after word, even though none registered within her brain. Sam sat next to her while they waited quietly, after spending what seemed like hours of writing answers, for the endocrinologist to study the questionnaire.

Dr. Gardner, the infertility specialist they had been sent to, scratched his beard thoughtfully before speaking. "If you've been trying to get pregnant for the last year and a half, we probably should schedule hormone tests for you, Sarah, and a semen analysis from you, Sam."

"What kind of tests are used?" Sarah asked.

"I'm going to request blood work to rule out non-reproductive disorders such as problems with the adrenal, pituitary or thyroid glands. You can do that at the lab after you're done here. If I find that inconclusive, I'll schedule a CC test. You'll take a prescription called clomiphene citrate so we can determine how your ovaries are responding to your body's hormone signals. From that test we can regulate your hormones."

Sarah glanced at Sam, trying to gage his feelings. She felt excited and scared at the same time. The role of becoming a mother might be as tenuous as becoming a wife, just a title which could be given to her and possibly much easier, be taken away from her. The doctor was describing tests she had never heard of. There was hope in what she did not understand, but they might also give conclusions she did not want.

"The next step would be to do a hysteron-salpingogram. That's an x-ray of the reproductive tract."

Sarah leaned forward in her chair. "What if either tests tell us nothing is wrong?"

The doctor leaned back in his chair and clasped his hands in front of him. "You really shouldn't worry about it until we get the initial test results back. Schedule the blood work and the semen analysis. The tests will tell us what direction we need to take so you will have a baby. There's in-vitro fertilization, zygote intrafallopian transfer, and intracytoplasmic sperm injections as options."

Sam reached out to take Sarah's hand. With his gesture of support, she molded her courage into words. "This is very important to us," Sarah spoke to the doctor hoping he would translate his list of technical words, which felt like a collection of official sounding names he had spent years gathering, into something reassuring.

The doctor glanced down at the paperwork again.

"On the family history, Sarah, you don't have anything written down," the doctor stated.

"You don't know any of the health history?"

"No, I was abandoned at the hospital. Neither parent could be tracked down."

"Well, I guess health history is secondary to these initial tests."

"You're hopeful Sarah could have a baby then?" Sam wanted the doctor to confirm.

"Sometimes couples won't have a baby for reasons we can't determine while others that have the odds against them, have babies. You can have hope, but you have to have faith too."

Faith, hope and love. Sarah thought of the bible verse that was repeated at their wedding. The most precious was love. The most precious would be a baby she could call her own. That would be the beginning of their family and it hurt to know she was so close to something she might never have.

As Sam drove away from the hospital complex, Sarah laid her head against the headrest of the car seat and closed her eyes. Negative thoughts swirled until there was a muddied sludge coating her emotions. There might never be a baby she could call her child, or hear it call her mother. She longed for this kind of possessiveness, not in the restrictive sense, but possessive as in belonging and the comfort of knowing one is connected to others in the world.

Growing up in foster care may have never given her the chance to belong, but there could have been other reasons that no one ever said out loud. She never did feel like she fit in with the white foster family she stayed with. But her dark skin was not dark enough to fit in with the African American foster families either. Everyone seemed to question her looks and with no one to blend in with, she belonged to no one. Sarah knew as well as the families that her time with them was transient.

As she got older, she would straighten her inherited African American hair with a curling iron, trying to look more like the white girls her age with straight hair. Later, the women in the African American foster homes taught her to use perm solutions to straighten her hair. That was something she would never have learned from a white foster mom. They would throw their hands up at the snarls in her hair, before she was taught to take care of her own hair. She had to learn to keep her opinions to herself and only later found the quiet approach worked best for her, being too dark in the mostly white communities and too light in the black communities.

She was sent to several different homes and seeing the same caseworker more than twice in a row was uncommon. They complained to her of being over loaded with cases. She tried to believe the inconsistency of workers may have been why she was never placed with an adoptive family and tried to give the ugly thoughts that maybe no one really wanted her limited access in her mind. She wanted to be valuable enough for anyone's permanent affections but was given the responsibility of taking care of fellow foster siblings when convenient for the foster parents. Because she grew up taking care of those smaller than she was, she developed a rapport with children. She attempted to offer the little ones a 'safe haven' of acceptance and care without resentment. This part of her personality most likely followed her into her profession as a physical therapist and made her good at what she did.

Out of high school, Sarah was given a small scholarship by a local church to attend community college. With excellent grades, she transferred to the nearby university and finished a professional degree in physical therapy. Working with children suffering from traumatic brain injuries was satisfying, but Sarah felt like she was still missing something.

Her thoughts migrated to the on again-off again romance with her first boyfriend, Lance. It had conveniently filled up the time while she attended college and before she had met Sam. With him, she first felt the possibility of belonging to a family. Lance had constantly talked about his family and she wanted so badly to be a part of it. But there was an inability for him to commit and Sarah was too afraid to ask him to define what their relationship was. It seemed that it had been easier for both of them to say nothing.

When she finally felt like she had nothing to gain, she found the confidence to leave everything she thought she wanted. When Lance introduced her with his heavy southern accent to his parents, she finally realized what she was losing by staying with him.

"Momma, Dad. This is my friend Sarah."

"Nice to meet you," Mrs. Tanner said in a genteel manner and held her hand out limply to Sarah. Mr. Tanner shook her hand quickly.

"It's a real pleasure to meet you," Sarah gushed, wanting them to like her. They sat down at the table with starched white linen table cloths and napkins folded into fans. Sarah felt uncomfortable with the formalness having grown up with the only white thing on the table being paper plates. Mrs. Tanner seemed to be right at home with the precisely laid forks, knife and spoons.

"Where your folks from, Sarah?" Mrs. Tanner asked.

"I don't know. I was abandoned at the hospital." There was no way to avoid telling the truth to nosey people, as they rooted around looking for conceptual history they acted entitled to.

"Well, I'm sure some nice family took you in."

"I was in foster care," Sarah had learned to say without emotion, presenting raw, an unpleasantness about this fact, hoping to stop further engaging questions.

"It's a shame to not know your roots," Mr. Tanner said. "We know our lineage all the way back to Scotland. Lance's momma has relations to the King of France, you know, before they killed him and his wife Marie Antoinette," he said, leaning over towards Sarah, like he was going to share a secret with her.

"He had a bit of a problem consummating that marriage. Ever since that, the women in that family have been looking for real men like us Tanner men."

"Don, that's not nice table talk," Mrs. Tanner said and then turned to Lance. "You should see Crissa Baker. We saw her at church last week. She's a beauty, Lance. You remember she was a few years younger than you growing up. She's home from college. You should come down and see her. She doesn't have a boyfriend."

"Aww, Momma. You make me blush."

Sarah felt her own cheeks flush in embarrassment. She recalled Lance had omitted saying girl and only called her a friend. They had broken up several times before, and now, being introduced to the family as a friend, she had officially become the in-between girl. She felt sadness creep over her as she recalled the stories he would tell her about his family. She was hungry for the closeness he described. Sarah was willing to overlook Lance's other girlfriends, if she could just have the chance to become a part of his family. It was the first time meeting his parents and she knew they would never accept her into their family and Lance would never commit.

"Where are you going?" Lance had asked her after dinner that night. His parents had retired to their hotel room.

"I'm leaving," Sarah said, standing at Lance's apartment door.

"But I want you to stay."

"I can't."

"Why? I want you to spend the night. What's the matter, baby?" he asked, putting his arms around her waist. He let go when she wouldn't return his embrace.

"It's tiresome to be the girl who gets called in between girlfriends. It's almost an expectation that I'll be there."

"You're reading more into this relationship."

"You're questioning my emotions?"

"Sarah, we're friends. I love you as a friend."

"I'm not a friend. You make love to me, but you won't admit that we are more than friends. I guess that's my fault. I continue to put myself in the position of ready and waiting. Eternally hopeful. Why am I not good enough to keep? You continually throw me away."

"Don't accuse me of that."

"I fantasize you're brave enough to love me like someone you want to spend your life with," she avoided looking into his eyes as she continued. "I know you love me, but you'll never commit to me. I'll never be a part of your family. You're weak."

"It's not like that."

"What is it then, Lance?" she pleaded.

"My family doesn't believe in mixed marriages. You have to understand where my family is from. Back in Macon, my family still raises the Confederate flag."

"But it's okay to have black friends? It's okay to have sex with black girls, but just don't marry them?" She refrained from yelling into his ears deafening accusations, *'Can't you see the white in me? Can't you see who I am on the inside?'*

"I know they're wrong, but I'd lose my whole family. I'd be abandoned. Don't you understand?"

"Yes, I do."

Sarah took his explanation more personally than him just being prejudice. She wondered if he found her skin so scary he couldn't be honest with their relationship. Because he was so afraid of what others would think, it made her feel not good enough, pretty enough, smart enough. Making him love her was a challenge. She tried so hard to prove she was worthy.

There were a few other relationships with different men, after breaking up with him, but none of them had any length or seriousness. Similar to Lance, they never understood or cared about her feelings. Each time she figured that out, she quit playing a part she thought each man wanted and would quietly withdraw, until there was nothing left.

She knew Sam loved her unconditionally, but there was no way he could understand how she truly felt. Sarah opened her eyes when Sam parked the car in their driveway. Like looking into a mirror, the windows of the house looked as empty as she felt inside. She felt him take her hand and squeeze it. Even if she could make him understand how she felt, it would not change what she was missing.

CHAPTER 11

The dawn had tinted the sky with pink. It would quickly fade as the sun rose and warmed the spring earth. Sarah gazed out the back windows of the house. The daffodils were almost finished, allowing the tulips their time to show off. She had gotten up to be with Sam when he had received the call, early in the morning. They had worked through a pot of coffee, waiting to call his sister. With a sigh, he dialed the phone.

"Hi Mike," Sam said into the phone after a few rings.

"Hey, Sam. You ready for this weekend? The fish are biting. Hope they still are when you come up," Mike's voice spoke out of the phone so loud that Sarah could hear him too, sitting across the kitchen table from Sam.

"Well Mike, I don't think that's going to work."

"You got something else going on?"

"I need to talk to Karen. Mom died last night."

"Oh, no. I'm so sorry Sam," Mike's jovial mood turned immediately somber. "Hold on a minute."

Sarah got up and poured fresh coffee into Sam's cup and then her cup.

"Hi Sam," Karen's voice came onto the phone.

"Hi Sis," Sam cleared his throat. "Mom passed away last night."

There was silence.

"Are you okay, Karen?" Sam asked.

"I don't know," she started. "I'm a little in shock."

"We knew this was going to happen. She had been getting weaker and weaker. Sarah said that Mom couldn't even say 'hi' the other day when she was there."

Karen did not respond, so Sam continued. "I'll be talking with the funeral home this morning. Was there anything that you wanted me to tell them?"

"I don't know right now. I'll call you if I think of something. When do you think the funeral will be?"

"They're not going to do it on Sunday," Sam considered. "Probably Monday or Tuesday."

"If we do it Monday, it might be better for people coming from out of town."

"I'll see what I can do."

"Are you going to stay with us?" Karen could be heard sniffing.

"Yes, if that's not a problem. We will probably leave this afternoon. We'll call when we leave."

"If you could call Mom's side of the family, we'll call Dad's side. That would help a lot."

"Okay. We'll see you tonight."

Sam clicked the phone off and sighed. Curls escaped as he ran his hand through his hair. Sarah stood at the kitchen sink, looking out the window with her arms crossed. Sam hung up the phone and went over to her.

"I'm sorry honey," Sam said, wrapping his arms around her. Sarah sighed and struggled out of his embrace.

"What are you thinking?" Sam asked.

"I don't know," Sarah said curtly and paced around the room. "She died alone. No one should have to do that."

"I don't think she was missing anyone's company. You spent a lot of time with her, in between my visits and my sister's visits."

"That's not what I mean," she shook her head back and forth with messy curls punctuating her discontent. "I wish that she could have stayed with us Sam."

"We both know she was a lot of care," Sam tried to reason with her.

"So, because she was high maintenance, we leave her with strangers?" Sarah knew what it was like to be cared for by workers and felt like she had let Laura down.

"That's not what I said."

"Karen was all for her going to the nursing home," Sarah accused. "Especially when I offered to let your mother live with us."

"You're reading things into what she said that aren't even true."

Sarah didn't respond. She remembered Karen saying "I know what's best for my mother."

"My mother is dead now. There's nothing we can change." Sam's voice quivered.

"I'm sorry, Sam. I loved her too. She was so good to me. I just wish that I could have done the same for her."

"You two really did hit it off."

"I guess." Guilt crept in, crowding out her feeling of loss because she had not acknowledged his. It had been his mother, the woman who had nurtured him ever since he was a baby and really, before he had even been born. Sarah had never had to consider mourning her mother, it was not like she could die when she did not exist as a person in her mind. There were more things to learn before she became a mother herself.

"I think she saw something in you."

"You might as well get started on your calls," Sarah said, brushing him away. "I'm going to start packing." She left the room leaving Sam looking out the window. Alone in the hall, tears ran down Sarah's face as she got the suitcases out of the closet. She would have welcomed her mother-in-law's sympathy, but Laura could not anymore. Sarah knew she would never be able to do that. She was gone.

There was relief and sadness traveling on the road to the nursing home. It would be the last time Sam and Sarah would need to go there and this trip was only to pick up Laura's belongings before they made their way north to Karen's. The funeral home had already taken Laura's body. For most of the ride they were both quiet and let the radio fill the silence that permeated the car.

"You don't have to come in," Sarah interrupted the radio. "I can do it."

"No, it's okay. I need to do it."

"I just didn't want this to be more painful than it is."

"It doesn't seem real. I knew it was going to happen, but I still can't believe she's gone."

"I know what you mean."

As they entered Laura's room, one of the nurse's aides was stuffing clothes into black garbage bags. Sam had already okayed her clothing to be donated to a local charity. The nursing aide who they recognized from past visits greeted them.

"I'm so sorry. We loved working with Laura," the girl said. Sam and Sarah mumbled thank you and stood awkwardly with their arms at their sides.

"Did you need something for her things?" the aide asked and tore off a black trash bag from the roll. "Go ahead. I can come back and get the rest of her clothes."

Sam took the bag while Sarah stepped to the other side of the bed and picked up a small plastic photo album on the bedside stand. She flipped through the pages of Karen and her family. She found her and Sam's wedding picture opposite Karen and Mike's anniversary picture. Laura probably looked at the pictures everyday as it sat out while the bible Karen had bought for Laura was in the drawer, Sarah discovered when she opened it. She smiled sadly, as she remembered Karen presenting Laura with the bible.

"You don't like it?" Karen's eyebrows arched.

"I didn't say that."

"There's nothing wrong with this one, Mom. It has Jesus and his twelve disciples in it plus Noah and all the animals. Why are you so hung up on that old ratty one?"

"Because it has all the names of my family in it."

"Are you afraid you'll forget their names?" Karen asked sarcastically.

"Maybe."

Sarah hid a smirk as she remembered Laura taking her aside and writing her name next to Sam's in the family bible. "There, you're part of the family," Laura had confirmed.

It had always been that way. Sarah remembered the first time she had met Sam's family. She had been afraid of them not accepting her, but hoped her fears would be wrong.

It was apparent that Laura tried hard to be thoughtful of Sarah, but stumbled on trying to do and say the right things. The comments had been uncomfortable and irritated Sarah, but she knew Laura was trying to ease Sarah's mind. It was not vindictive or sheer curiosity that Laura used like some people would do while gawking at the animals at the zoo. No way would they want them in their house, only the familiar cat or dog would do. She wished she could have explained to Laura that having black skin could feel as fragile as glass, but pointing out her own differences would only give her less validity to being part of the family, a part of something that did not look like her.

But after that first dinner with the family, none of them brought the subject up. It seemed like Sam's family just looked but avoided the word. It was like a game. Everyone knew the word and all the words that were associated with it, but they all had to pretend it did not exist.

Sarah had long forgiven Laura and wondered about her determination of giving her daughter's shoes away to a girl with a different color of skin when Karen had not been done with them. A smile crept across Sarah's face as she appreciated this idea she had in her head, of Laura keeping secrets.

Sam and Sarah finished gathering pictures, cards and a few books and put them in a garbage bag to take home. It seemed cruel to do that, making Laura's life unimportant by putting her last material possessions into a trash bag. Sarah knew there was more to the life Laura had lived which could not be summed up in the hodgepodge they were hauling away. A trash bag was a thing used to hold things meant to be thrown away. They left the nursing home, carrying the last memories of Laura's life. Those memories would not be thrown out, no matter how old or shabby they became. Sarah would cherish them.

The fresh air cleared Sarah's head of the potent smell of lily's and other aromatic flowers from the arrangements that surrounded Laura's casket at the funeral. Little magnetic flags waved to each other from the top of the cars. The men in dark suits respectfully waved their arms at Sam and Sarah, guiding them to the car at the front of the procession. The headlights were barely visible in the bright sunshine as the hearse carrying Laura's casket led the way to the cemetery on the other side of town. Following the hearse was the black limo provided by the funeral home. Sam and Sarah rode backwards, facing Mike and Karen.

"What do you think Mom would have thought of us riding in such high class?" Sam asked lightheartedly. He met with Karen's look of disapproval from the comment.

"She was a very classy lady," Sarah offered, meaning it sincerely.

Mike worked at forming his smile of amusement at Sam into a frown of concern for Karen.

"This is respectful, Sam," Karen scolded.

Sam pouted and looked out the back window directly between Karen and Mike and watched the line of vehicles grow behind them.

"You don't remember what Mom said when Dad died," Sam said, more as a statement than a question.

Karen looked at him. "Which thing?"

"She said funerals are for the living. We don't have to act dead because she is."

Karen started crying. Sarah did too. She now had someone to mourn.

"It's sad, Karen," Sam choked on his words. "We're all going to miss her. I need her as much as you do."

Silence fell to the inside of the car. Sarah ached for the woman she had grown to love. The hurt was so intense. She could feel empathy for Karen, almost forgiving her for the usual barbed comments, insinuating Sarah was not part of their family.

Sarah finally spoke. "I remember the first time I met her. She acted like she had known me forever."

"She did take an immediate liking to you," Sam said to Sarah and put his hand over hers.

"I remember when she scared me into turning the light off at night when I was a kid," Sam recalled. "She stood outside my bedroom window, knowing full well that I was reading a Hardy Boys book. When she knocked on the glass, the neighbors a mile away heard my screaming."

Mike started laughing until tears ran down his face.

Karen spoke. "I remember when she and Dad use to take us to the stream. We'd have a picnic lunch and play and fish all day."

Sarah watched Sam smile broadly at his sister. Karen would be alright. So would Sam. Sarah wanted to feel the same reassurance that she would be alright too without Laura's comforting guidance.

CHAPTER 12

Laura had been waiting for this moment for a long time. Now that she was dead, she no longer had aches and tiredness that accumulated more weight each day as if she had the strength to carry it as it grew. She felt young again, knowing what it was not just to think but feel a freedom born of naivety. When she was alive, it seemed like her spirit had aged slower than her body aged chronologically. It felt good to have the two back in sync again.

She ultimately had no choice in her death, so she accepted the fortune of youth she was given and grieved that she would not watch her grandchildren grow up or offer support to her children, even though Karen and Sam were adults and able to take care of themselves. There even was an unmistakable feeling of missing Sarah.

Sam's wife was so charming. She adored this girl and loved how Sarah could stop Sam in his tracks when he started getting intense. Laura had developed a friendship with Sarah that lasted up to the time that she fell ill and couldn't converse with her the same way. Sarah was so patient and did not make her feel ashamed when her memory failed. Sarah never seemed to tire of hearing the family stories over and over. Laura would miss her. She was part of the family now.

The white clapboard church where she married Peter and baptized her children filled up with people and noise. The adults called to each other, exchanging greetings and gossip while the younger kids found this experience as another opportunity to have fun and chased each other until reprimanded. Toddlers and babies cooed and tested the echoes created by the high ceilings in the sanctuary with their own language.

Laura had not seen this many people in reunion since her husband had died ten years ago. The ones that had passed away since had been replaced with the new faces of small children and babies. It was hard to believe that her family was this big and all these people had come to pay their last respects to her.

"Look, it's Barb and Ted," Laura said, pointing to the woman hunched over and pushing a man in a wheelchair. "I haven't seen them in ages."

Her mother nodded in acknowledgment.

"There's Matthew," she whispered is surprise, recognizing him through the white hair and thick glasses.

"Those have to be Phil and Donna's kids," she mused, as that generation had become versions of their parents when they were that age.

It was like no other family reunion she had been to where she could see those who had preceded her in death and those who were still very much alive. It was so much more than what she dreamed death might be. She was a part of each family member who was there, yet she could not wait to experience what it would be like to see, to touch and to talk to her loved ones again. She wondered if they would remember who she was.

But Laura did not fully understand what death meant until she went to touch a loved one who passed near her. Her mother drew her hand back.

"You can't do that anymore," Rose informed her.

Laura looked imploringly at her mother. It was the first time she had felt anguish since she had passed into death.

"I know," Grandfather Levi sympathized. "At first it's very painful."

Laura slowly tried to make sense of her new knowledge. To have both, the loved ones who had left before her and the ones who she left behind, was impossible. She tried to conceal her disappointment while she watched in silence as more people came in and people greeted each other.

"Do you hear how many times your name is being said?" Grandfather Levi whispered to her. "They are really remembering you. Look at your family. Look at your friends." He pointed in reference. "You were really rich with love."

"That's a wonderful thing," the composure of her voice waivered. "But why do I feel so sad?"

"Because this is good-bye for you. This is good-bye for them."

"But after this, they won't forget me, will they?" Laura asked, looking for reassurance. "I don't want to be forgotten."

"That's the way most feel at first," Rose said. "They reunite with those that were forgotten and feel that they too will become forgotten and unknown over time also. You have to remember you helped create the future."

"Look at that baby over there," Grandfather Levi pointed. "That little boy. You won't be forgotten. There's a part of you in that boy. You will continue to live on, even when that little boy has babies of his own," he promised.

"How do you know that he's one of mine?" Laura asked with surprise.

"I know. I've been watching over him, like I did with his father. I know that's Karen's grand-baby." Grandfather Levi stated. Laura looked thoughtful, absorbing the whole idea of watching over someone.

"You will watch over someone too." Rose said to Laura, seeing her daughter trying to comprehend what that meant.

"How will I know who that is?" Laura asked.

"Watch today. See who needs your love, more so, now that you are gone. Today will be very important for you," her mother said with Grandfather Levi nodding his head in agreement.

Laura watched as she stood beyond the group of mourners who crowded around the hole in the cemetery. As the casket was lowered into the grave, loved ones she had left behind said their last good-byes. It felt odd to Laura to watch them shed tears over the pine box that held only her body. Her death was becoming more and more real and less of a dream. She stole glances back at the living as she followed behind her mother and Grandfather Levi.

CHAPTER 13

The ride from the funeral home to the cemetery had been lighthearted, but with the casket of his mother sitting next to the hole, the heaviness of grief pulled Sam's head down. Guilt ran in a continuous loop in his mind, even though he knew he had been a good son. He could have been better. Wishing for his mother to still be alive was silly, but he wanted more of her, a chance to make sure he listened this time to all of her stories. Anger at himself mingled with the guilt as he wished he had when he had the chance.

Sam was a child where death did not pervade his growing up. It was something he had not spent much time thinking about. When they drove past the funeral home in town, he did not consciously think of its purpose. He was able to live in the moment. His mind was preoccupied with what he was going to do, how he was going to do it and when he was going to do it. His focus was not on the end or what the world might be like without him. Even in his first decisions as an adult, there had not been room for those thoughts when he had so much to accomplish.

The fall of his senior year at college he began dating a girl named Linda. On weekends they would go across the street from the university and have dinner and catch a movie with the money he earned from his part-time job at the bowling alley in the basement of the Student Union. Life was good for him as the draft was over and job offers were being made.

That spring he invited Linda to lunch for his birthday when his family came down. He did not think it was a big deal until after his family left and he and Linda walked along the river. It was early spring and the daffodils were in bloom. As they approached the Alumni Chapel, Linda hinted about being married there. Sam was surprised but also uncomfortable thinking he might have to slow down for commitment when he had so much he wanted to do.

"I'm too young and too busy to settle down right now," he said, hoping she would drop the talk of marriage.

"At least you're honest about being selfish," her voice waivered, as if she wanted to be strong against his rejection.

"You can call it what you like. I'm not ready yet."

"Will you ever be ready?"

"Don't wait for me," he said bluntly.

"I wasn't asking for me. It was rhetorical."

"Don't you want to see the world?" his arms waved to emphasize the passion in his voice. "Don't you want to do things free people can do? I have the rest of my life to be bored with a wife and family."

"I pity that woman."

"Look, I don't want to be like my parents or their parents. All the stories I've heard about their lives was about the struggles they went through being married and being a parent. Only my Great Grandmother Julia talked about how she wished she had done more, anything, something with her life before she had settled down."

"You've just lived the college experience."

"No, I've just spent the last four years of my life worrying about carrying a rifle rather than textbooks."

"But that's over, you have to move on."

"The draft is over, but my career is just starting."

The Library loomed next to the river and they turned and cut across the field, cris-crossed with sidewalks until they were standing under the shadow of Beaumont Tower, where the bells pealed out the noon hour every day.

"Good-bye, Sam," Linda said, stepping away from him.

"I'm sorry I feel the way I do."

"Me too," she said and walked towards her dorm.

He headed back to his own dorm room at the ivy covered Mason-Abbott Hall and felt the chill of the night air as the sun set. He did not intend to hurt her like that, but he could not agree to share his life at the expense of his own dreams. Maybe if Linda came through his life again in another five years or so, there would be room for her. It was quite possible she would find someone who was willing to be married right away. In his mind he justified any of the hurt feelings he may have caused and hoped for her own happiness.

As a fresh engineering graduate from Michigan State, Sam was hired at a metal fabrication and heat treatment plant back in his home town. Sam took the teasing from friends that he had found a job working in heavy metal. But he did not care what they said, his goal was to show the world a self made man.

Five or so years of working his way up in the company and casually dating passed quickly and it was at that point he realized Linda had been a darling. Smart, funny, all the right clichéd things anyone would want in a girl friend. Now that he was ready for her, there were no women he seemed to be attracted to. He worked at the plant fifty to sixty hours a week with a workforce that was almost exclusively male, sans the receptionist who was married and had two children. There were no women to be friends with and he was reluctant with 'set ups' by good intentioned coworkers. All of the 'eligible' girls, who were still around in his home town, had married and had kids while he had been away to college. Some of them were even working on their first divorce.

Then he met Audrey. She was bossy and always had to get her way. He fell head over heels in lust over her looks. She was beautiful. She wanted to do things in life, passionate about the rewards and fun, like Sam. But perhaps he had misread the passion until he had spent a few years in marriage with her.

They moved back to the big city of his college years and started their newlywed life fighting over money constantly, it seemed like. She was determined she was not going to live like they were poor. They were far from it, but her definitions of comfortable were new cars every other year because she got bored with them, jewelry and leather coats and fur coats charged to accounts because money went to buying a new house. Even with cash being short after paying bills, she insisted on entertaining with lots of food and alcohol and eventually drugs. When he told her to slow down, she became displeased.

"We should really be thinking about saving some money for college if our kids are ever going to go."

"Maybe those are your priorities, but they aren't mine. I work too hard for my money and I deserve to spoil myself."

"It's my money too that you're spending and I say you can't keep spending like this."

"I'm not changing anything."

"That's what you think."

"No, you had your chance to be successful, but you don't want to. There's no other alternative but divorce," she informed him.

Relief seemed a bigger winner than any fear of losing her. For most of his life he was able to be selfish, where he was putting himself first, but not at the expense of others, at least he thought. He liked being a young man not wanting responsibilities of family. Audrey had made him aware of what real selfishness was.

Standing at the edge of his mother's grave, thinking about his old girlfriend and ex-wife did he realized what he was doing to Sarah. He had already lost two women, or more so, a case of going through them, and he felt worn out to think he might have to go through it again. But his thinking had to change, he had to support Sarah, otherwise he might lose her too.

Perhaps that was the reason why he was unable to understand Sarah's obsession of wanting to create something that would be a part of her. Being nurtured within the palisades of his family, he felt little threat about not knowing who he was. He always had very straightforward roles, a son, a brother, as a husband. Those roles meant something and were important to him. Sarah did not have that and maybe that is why he saw her focus on having a baby an obsession.

He pulled Sarah into his embrace as the minister called them into prayer for the last time.

Maybe Sam had not listened carefully to his mother's stories because he had been more interested in making his own. There was a pleasant feel of familiarity in this woman he had been ready to marry and was now ready to have children with. This time he was committed, he was ready to keep Sarah. He was ready to make new stories with Sarah in his life.

CHAPTER 14

Laura had found a grassy spot near the bank of the river. This place had held importance when she was alive. She always hated to leave the comforting whisper of pine, spruce and deciduous leaves accompanying the babble of the river. While beckoning to come closer, to see where it lived, hoping to tease anyone looking at it with sun pennies glinting on the ever changing flow of water, Laura knew it would continue moving, telling her the same things when she returned.

She had first come here with her husband before they had married and visited often with a basket of lunch provisions, and later with babies in tow. The last time she had been there was when the kids were young teens. They had been fishing with their father for sunfish and the little, sweet tasting blue gills.

Laura's white hair had gotten so brittle and thin in the nursing home. Now it was hanging down around her shoulders in soft dark brown waves, created from her hair being braided tightly. She felt her face and couldn't detect the deep wrinkles that had formed on her forehead and around her eyes. There was a firmness and resiliency to her full cheeks. Only the creases at her knuckles broke the smoothness of her soft hands. These were the hands before she had married Peter, borne him children and scrubbed infinite pots and pans, floors and laundry.

Perhaps this was the point in her life that she had been the freest. The physical age that she continued to carry in her heart and mind. No matter what image the mirror reflected, she had always felt the youth deep inside herself that longed to run as fast as she could across the meadow. The youth of eating crisp apples warmed by the sun and so juicy that the sweetness ran down your chin. Being young enough to wipe the trickles of juice away from your mouth with the back of your sleeve when no one else was around. Or the eternally youthful feeling that came from the spring breeze that smelled like earth with a hint of sweetness picked up from the early spring blossoms.

She ran her fingers through a few long blades of grass, feeling the coolness that the shade had created. The clean scent of pine was always underfoot and the ferns waved in the under-story. The sunlight worked its way past the limbs and leaves and dappled the ground. Afternoon naps on the partially shaded river banks were more restful than an entire night of sleep in bed. Memories flitted through her mind like the new leaves that fluttered in the breeze. Another shadow appeared near where she was sitting. Laura looked up and smiled at the man standing over her.

"Peter," Laura said in acknowledgment. She was sure that she could smell the honest and hardworking smells of dirt and sawdust on him as he knelt down and sat beside her.

"I thought I might find you here," he said. "I heard that you were going to be with us. I started out this way as soon as I heard. I'm sorry I didn't make it sooner."

Laura looked at him not fully understanding. "Where are you now?" she asked.

"I went back to North Carolina to be with my family. I went to look after my little sister. Plus, that is really home to me."

"I'm surprised," she said trying to comprehend what he was saying.

"Why is that?" He said and sat down next to Laura.

"I'm surprised that you didn't stay with us. But I guess it makes sense."

"Your mother watched over you. You didn't need me anymore."

Laura wondered if she had not needed Peter after he died and that was something he had known all along. She did not realize her mother had been watching over her. It left her with a feeling of surprise. While they sat next to each other, Laura remembered this was how Peter looked when he was her young husband. He combed his hair through his fingers, releasing the sandy blond curls.

Later in life they had turned grey and then white, but it had never thinned.

His muscles were heavy with strength that rippled beneath the shirt he was wearing. Being a farm boy had defined his physical brawniness. Peter had come to Northern Michigan during the Great Depression to work on his uncle's farm. He was able to work for room and board and the smallest amount of pay each month which he sent back home to his family. Peter had made the choice to leave his childhood home in North Carolina so that there was one less mouth to feed.

It nearly broke Laura's heart with worry when Peter went to Europe during World War II. Peter came back and they began their married life with Laura taking care of the house and garden and Peter taking a job at the local foundry while playing gentleman farmer on the weekends. When the children came, joy was theirs, but she also remembered their fights.

Peter broke her thoughts. "Did you live life the way you wanted?" he asked.

"I think I did. With what we had available. We lived a hard life. Working hard, that is. Worrying about having enough to feed the kids. At the time I felt bad that we couldn't give our children new toys and new clothes all the time," she sighed. "Looking back though, we gave them a work ethic and a good moral character. Those are things money can't buy. We gave them a lot of love and space to explore. We did the best with what we had. I did the best I could."

"I wish I could have been able to provide you an easier life." Peter looked at her intensely. "You really deserved more than you got."

"I don't know how you could have. We both worked as hard as we could." There really wasn't any answer to the truth that Laura spoke. They both sat in silence for a few minutes. Reminiscing of the past with each other during the silence was likely, but more so, it seemed to allow them to continue skirting the issue of being good to each other as husband and wife.

"Did you live life the way you wanted?" Laura asked Peter back. "I know that you never spoke it. But I think that you wished to live and farm back in North Carolina."

"I guess I lived life the best way possible. I would never have thought that afterwards I'd get to go back home, so things did work out."

It still made Laura feel funny when Peter referred to back home and she knew that it wasn't there with her.

Peter must have noticed the hurt Laura's face expressed.

"I hope that you can understand why I call North Carolina home."

Laura smiled, trying to disguise her emotions.

"I have no regrets in marrying you Laura. I have no regrets in raising our children together. I don't even have regrets about never returning to North Carolina while I was alive. I had committed myself in marriage to you, for better or worse. I loved you Laura."

'Do you not love me now?' Laura thought. She didn't ask because she comprehended their relationship had changed again, with more distance separating them. They had stayed married and faithful to each other. Laura never had a relationship with any other man after that. Their children had buried them both at the cemetery by the lake. For their children, Laura and Peter lay side by side for eternity.

"I'm going to go and see the children before I return to North Carolina," he said.

"They're doing beautifully," Laura said slowly, hoping that she would say the right things if she paced herself. "I'm sorry for saying that you weren't a good father. I was mad at you. I didn't think it was right for you to be involved with such a hateful group," she hurried to say before she lost her chance and her courage. "I didn't want to raise our children like that. I was scared."

"I did the best I could to take care of my family." Peter said quietly and gave Laura a pleading look. "I had beliefs and I did what you wished. I kept them to myself. We're dead now. I don't have anything else to prove to you."

"The children have always thought that you were a good father," Laura said. "I burned your robes after you died. I didn't want Karen or Sam finding them." She dared to feel proud of keeping his secret from their children. Their secret. It would only create pain and confusion for them if they knew.

"Thank you," Peter said.

"What did you think when Sam brought Sarah home?" Laura asked bluntly.

"Will you ever forgive me, Laura?"

"Perhaps, but can I forgive myself for allowing it?" she said more for herself.

"We can't change what has happened." Peter seemed impatient as he leaned over and kissed her forehead. "It was good to see you, Laura."

"Take care of yourself," Laura said.

Peter left silently the way he came.

She sat with a dizzy feeling, thinking about the young lady she had been before she had met her husband. She knew she would marry and raise children, so the decision to marry Peter was not a rash or surprise choice. Deep inside Laura's inner most thoughts, she had questioned if that was her only destiny. Laura now saw that he was not her only choice, but the best choice. Peter had been a good father and husband. She and Peter had been married for almost forty years. They had been good parents to their children. That is all.

CHAPTER 15

Rose sat on the beach alone. The sky was overcast in grey and the air smelled green. Some might call it a fishy smell, but it was very faint and it came and went with the wind blowing fresh air off of the lake. The waves lapped at the shore forcefully but with melancholy, trying to entice one with its rhythm to continue listening to its sadness. It was a never ending sob of loneliness which became louder as one approached and diminished in its will to pull you in as one got further from the forlorn story it wanted to tell.

There were certain stories Rose could not quit remembering. After she died, she finally acquiesced to let them run their course each time they started in her mind, believing she might figure them out eventually. She knew the story of when she first hated her mother, Julia, and little sister, Lily. But it still haunted her to make sense of it.

With a child's quest, Rose had slipped into her parent's room to look at Mother's doll. She told herself she would only look at it while Mother was hanging laundry outside to dry and Lily was playing in the yard. But Rose could not resist picking up the doll and cradling it gently in her arms. In the heat of summer air, Rose loved feeling the cool sensation of the doll's porcelain face against her cheek. Mother loved this doll. Mother rarely smiled, but when she dusted gently around the doll she would tell stories of being a little girl in New York and her lips would form a smile and her eyes would echo as she squinted, turning into upside down smiles. Rose loved the doll for how it transformed Mother. She had been told to never play with the doll, but she could not resist sneaking into her parent's room and holding it.

A sound at the doorway made Rose look up to see Lily step into the room.

"You're not allowed to touch the doll," Lily whispered.

"Go away, Lily. I'm putting her back."

"I want to hold her first," Lily said, grabbing at the doll.

"Let go," Rose hissed at her sister and tried to release the doll from Lily's grasp.

"I want to hold her too."

"No, you'll break her. Let go," Rose said and reached out to push Lily away. With Rose's loosened grip, Lily was able to pull the doll out of Rose's hands.

"You give her back," Rose demanded, taking a step forward. She watched Lily holding the doll by its legs and swinging it toward her. The doll head hit her in the nose and a lightning bolt of pain shot through her face. Rose watched Lily's mouth fall open and eyes explode with fear. She dropped the doll on the floor and started shrieking as she fled the room. Rose chased after her, where Lily's screams turned into intelligible calls for their mother.

Rose had run down the steps and into the kitchen in pursuit of Lily, when she stopped suddenly and cupped her hands around her nose. Pulling them away, she saw the bright red of barn paint marking her hands. It was not paint but blood. That was when Mother burst through the door with Lily grabbing at her skirts, crying.

"Lord have mercy," Mother yelled as she grabbed Rose up in her arms. Rose started crying. She let her mother lead her to the sink and start to clean her face. Rose now felt the extent of the pain associated with the doll's head cracking into her nose and cutting a wide gash. She let her mother care for her, a gentleness that was usually void when her mother interacted with her. Rose tried not to squirm and let her mother clean the cut on the bridge of her nose and pinch her nostrils closed so the bleeding would stop from the inside. She was a big girl, but sat with her mother in the rocking chair and let her mother sooth her. "I love you, my pretty baby," her mother whispered into her ear. Lily skulked around the room and kept watching them.

Mother had Rose lay on the davenport when the bleeding had subsided. Rose relaxed while her mother busied herself in the kitchen as Father would be home soon for dinner. Lily stayed in the room with Rose but they did not speak to each other. Rose was dozing off when she heard her mother shriek. It was not from the kitchen but from upstairs. Rose bolted to a sitting position. Mother came stomping down the stairs holding the doll in one hand and the pieces of broken off face in the other.

"What on earth happened to my doll?" Mother hollered at the girls.

"Rose did it," Lily burst out.

"What do you mean Rose did it?"

"No, I didn't. Lily did it," Rose defended.

"I saw Rose playing with it," Lily confirmed.

Rose went cold as she watched her mother march across the room and grab her up by the arms.

"How could you break my doll? How dare you touch her. You've been told not to touch her," Mother screamed as she viciously shook Rose back and forth. Lily sank to the floor and covered her ears with her hands and gave out piercing shrieks.

"No, I didn't," Rose cried and wiggled free of her mother's grip. "No, I didn't."

Rose felt her mother grab the braid that hung down her back and fell to the floor and her mother's fists immediately pummeled against her body.

Over the din of Lily's incessant wailing, Rose screamed, "No, Mother, don't," answering her mother's repeated rant "How could you?" over and over.

Rose cried tears of hurt. She did not feel the pain of her bloodied nose or where her mother struck her, but in the soft spots where her mother had briefly shown her affection and was now accusing her. The slap of the back door was hardly noticed.

"What is going on?" Rose heard her father bellow. She no longer felt her mother's fists and looked up to see that her father had grabbed Mother off of her.

"She broke my doll. She broke my doll," Mother screamed out the indignity of the trespass as Father held her fast in his arms until she went limp. Father released his grip on her and she proceeded to walk out the door. Rose watched her mother's slumped figure heading for the barn.

"Rose, honey," Father said softly, picking her up. "What happened?"

Rose buried her face in her father's chest and when she pulled away, she saw the blood on his shirt. Lily had silently sidled up to them.

"I didn't mean to," Rose whispered.

"You girls know how much that doll means to your mother," he stated. They shook their heads up and down in understanding.

"You can help get Rose cleaned up," he said to Lily. "I'm going to check on your mother."

Without exchanging a word, they washed the blood off of Rose's face again and then went to the bedroom. They heard their father coaxing their mother into the house and to their bedroom. Rose lay on her bed with her eyes closed but could still feel Lily's presence across the room, weighing heavy like a putrid scent coming from the pustulated decay that seemed to be eating at the edges of her soul. A little while later their father came to the bedroom and had them come out to the kitchen to eat a supper of bread and fried eggs. After they were done, Father went to check on Mother, and Rose washed the dishes while Lily dried them. The soapy bubbles hid Rose's hands while she washed the plates and felt their warmness from sitting in the hot water.

Rose stayed mad at Lily for the half truth she had told her parents. To bring the subject up again days later to indict Lily was not worth it to Rose. She held her grudge against Lily even after Father had carefully glued the doll's face together. The crack on the dolls forehead was as obvious as the scar forming on the bridge of Rose's nose.

Rose felt guilty about her mother's own sorrows, but hated Lily more. Even when it felt like Mother was personally attacking her, Rose blamed it on Lily. A child's logic could not imagine a mother being repulsed by her own child and refusing to love was akin to starving a baby of mother's milk.

It had been ritual on Sunday mornings when Mother was getting ready for church, Rose and Lily would clamor for a dusting on their noses too. In the mirror, the reflection of the three showed the aged beauty of Mother, Lily's delicate features that promised her mother's beauty and the coarse angularness of Rose's face. Mother tapped the powder puff lightly on Lily's nose and then turned to Rose to do the same.

"No powder is going to make that nose smaller," Rose heard her mother say. "You get that from your father." Indeed, she had inherited his facial features and his prominent nose. Only hers had the scar running across the bridge.

"Rosey with the big nosey," Lily started chanting.

Tears welled up in Rose's eyes.

"Don't cry. It'll make your nose run," Mother scolded. "Don't need to draw any more attention to that nose."

When Mother dusted around the doll she no longer smiled. Lily asked her season's later to tell her a story about New York as she dusted around the faded taffeta dress.

"Not anymore, Lily," Mother sighed. "The only thing this doll reminds me of now is of broken dreams."

Rose's dislike of Lily grew and grew each day. Lily did not need her love, Rose justified, when she had their parents. She daydreamed about what her life would have been like if Lily had never been born. Then she could have slipped into her parent's room and held the doll and rubbed her cheek against the cool porcelain any time she had wanted.

Rose would still sneak in and hold the doll, but was more careful. "I love you, my pretty baby,"

Rose would whisper to the doll and pretend it was her mother saying it to her.

The scar on the bridge of her nose was erased with the fantasy of no Lily. To wish premature death on her only sibling was wrong, but Rose could not help thinking her mother would have to love her if Lily was gone.

At thirteen, Rose became the only child that she wanted to be. Mother became sick, then Lily. Rose tried to take care of them the best she could, until she got sick too. Father took over nursing them back to health. Mother recovered and then Rose, but Lily's fevers lingered and then the fluid collected in her lungs until she could not breathe anymore. Rose felt guilt for wishing her sister dead. She knew she had not made it happen, but was still afraid her bad thoughts somehow had been heard.

It was while people visited the house with Lily's simple casket on display in the front room of the house did Rose overhear guests murmur quietly how sad it was Julia's pretty daughter had died. She knew then, her mother would never love her the way she wanted her to.

In all of her mother's vanity, Rose was surprised at her mother's willingness to be called Grandmother Julia. Laura's birth had transformed the once stately woman into a gracious older lady. She watched her daughter, Laura, seeing how much grandmother and granddaughter were alike with their smiling upside down eyes and delicate features. With the birth of Laura, her mother's hopes of life in New York were rekindled. The smiles returned. She watched her mother dote on Laura, knowing she was immaturely feeling jealousy of the relationship between her mother and her daughter.

When Laura had been born, Julia had curled her lip. "A baby girl. Well, let us hope she's blessed with some looks." Rose seethed at her mother's accusations that she wasn't pretty. Harry had been such a wrinkly, red baby. Laura seemed to glow. She was already a pretty baby.

As Laura grew to feed herself and toddle, Rose watched her mother shower her affections on that pretty child. It hurt to think that Rose had never been pretty enough for her mother's attention. Laura had been blessed with her grandmother's beauty and would look up at Grandmother Julia, mirroring her smiling eyes.

Rose remembered following her mother into the bedroom to look at a new dress she had bought. Laura, with her little legs, ran ahead, knowing that a visit to the bedroom was a chance to hold the doll. She climbed up on the bed and sat waiting for Grandmother Julia to bring it to her.

Rose waited with clenched teeth while her mother got the doll for Laura and bitterly recalled how the smile from her mother's lips and eyes had disappeared the day she and Lily had fought over the doll. That had also been the last day her mother had touched her. She tried to imagine those shaky hands with knobs of arthritis being child's hands at one time, but she only saw the creped skin balled up in fists and pummeling her body. Her mother held the doll so gingerly to protect its fragility, yet the doll was broken despite the glue, yellowed from age, holding the face together.

Her mother, who had developed a permanent stooped posture from old age, did not even need to bend over to place the doll in Laura's outstretched arms. Julia had become so old Rose could not imagine her as a young girl or a young woman. The hair, the skin, the padding in all the wrong spots, disguised the beauty that once graced the bones of the now slumped skeleton. Rose wondered if when she looked in the mirror, she remembered herself.

"All the way from France to New York. She traveled all that way for my seventh birthday," her voice wavered with a hint of oncoming tears. "And then she traveled with me to Michigan."

Rose had heard her mother tell this story thousands of times and heard her tell Laura hundreds of times. This time Laura asked a question.

"How did her face get broken?"

Rose held her jaw tighter. No one had uttered the reason since the day Lily had shouted "She did it."

"You will have to ask your mother that," Rose heard her mother say and watched her eyes rise to meet hers with a look of satisfaction.

"Mamma?" Laura asked, smoothing out the doll's hair.

Rose did not answer her daughter. She had no words to describe how she felt about her mother loving that doll more than she.

"Sometimes when we break, we think it's all over, but there's always hope," Grandmother Julia said and cupped Laura's face in her gnarled hands and smiled with her eyes.

Rose put a fist up to hide her tears, but her mother saw them.

"Oh, Heaven's to Betsy," Grandmother Julia said. "Don't start crying. Your water works don't get my sympathy."

Rose was mad at Laura for asking, even though it had been innocent. Now, years of replaying this scene over and over, she recalled hoping her mother never hurt Laura like she had done to her. But Rose had never been able to overcome her fear of Laura and ended up hurting her anyways.

Tired of reliving her regrets, she listened for other voices in her memory. Happy voices of children playing in the water. In her mind's eye she saw her precious children, Harry, Laura and Little Andrew playing as she watched the children from the shore and periodically shouted at the children to be careful or play nicely.

A hand on her shoulder broke her daydream of the broken doll and the children playing on the beach. Rose looked at the hand and then up to her daughter's face.

"You're remembering Little Andrew before he died." Laura stated in a matter of fact tone and sat down next to her. This was the beach were Little Andrew drowned.

"You're right. I've been here hundreds of times, trying to find answers for the questions I had when I was alive, trying to release my guilt. " Rose said pulling her skirt taut around her ankles, attempting to keep the breeze from chilling her legs underneath. "I've been reunited with him and I've told him how much I love him and how much I've missed him, but I keep thinking about the life he could have had. Why didn't I do anything to save him?"

"Does it get any better?" Laura asked in an empathetic tone.

Rose mulled over the question before answering. "I've come to realize even in my death and being with my son once again, I still have to come here and relive it over and over. I've finally been able to leave here with a little more peace in my heart each time I come."

Regardless of years or even death, Rose would never forget holding her new baby in the crook of her arm. Another boy. She inhaled the new baby smell and her fingertips glided over the soft smooth skin. Her third baby. There was Harry, Laura and now Little Andrew. She knew the only reason they had three children was because James liked sex, so much, she knew he had been finding other women the last few months before Little Andrew was born to do what she could not. She dared not to look too close at any of the children in town. She never wanted to recognize one as her husband's.

But he was a decent father, Rose made herself believe. He treated the children well, talked to them when they were bad instead of switching them and rarely let the children witness his behavior after drinking. He usually slept it off in someone else's bed. But James told her time and time again, she was lucky to have him and then he would run his finger across the scar of her nose, to remind her that she would be hard pressed to catch another man's eye. Her plain face was broken up by the scar and swollen belly would quickly become soft and flabby. Nor would any other man tangle with a feisty scrap of a man, such as James.

No, leaving James was not a possibility. She had nowhere to go. Her parent's home was not even a possibility. Her mother doted on Laura, but to have to care for her and have her underfoot, that would not happen. Rose would rather endure the humiliation of her husband's infidelity than her mother's proclamations of 'you're not the pretty one. No man would have you now.' Rose was sure her mother would not say that in so many words, but she could feel it in the sharpness of the tone her mother took with her.

James would come around. If she stayed loyal and encouraged him, he might see that she was valuable. He was so insecure of his height and Rose felt sorry for him. With his children he could feel like a man, towering over them and for once not having to physically raise his head to acknowledge a world where everyone seemed taller than he.

"You don't love me because I'm short," he would taunt her with guilt. "I'm just as much a man as any of them I see you looking at when were in town. Don't know why you're looking. They wouldn't have you, you're a momma now," he could say and poke at her swollen belly.

Rose and Laura sat in silence for a while. They heard voices and footsteps on the boardwalk that led from the present day parking lot to the beach. Neither the boardwalk, the playground or the parking lot were in existence when Laura visited here with her family decades ago. They watched a little boy, about the age of Little Andrew when he died, run to the edge of the water with his blue plastic bucket swinging from his hand.

"Christian," The woman called from the boardwalk. "Wait for me and your father."

The boy didn't seem too concerned with waiting as he started squatting in the sand and picked up pebbles and put them into his bucket. Each went into the bucket with a plunk sound as it hit the plastic bottom.

His parents finally caught up to him and immediately both shifted their gaze downwards.

Occasionally they would bend down and pick up a pebble and call to their son to put it in his bucket.

"Is this one a Petosky?" The boy asked his father.

His father looked at the pebble for a moment.

"No, I think that's an agate. We're a little far south to find Petosky's."

The little boy resumed picking up rocks.

"I'm freezing," The woman said. "How much longer?"

"Go back to the car," The man said. "I'll stay here. We'll only be a few more minutes."

Laura and Rose continued watching the father and his son. After the woman left the little boy started throwing rocks into the lake. Going back in time several decades, it could have been Little Andrew on the beach with Harry.

"Try this flat one," The man said handing his son a flat stone. "See if you can skip it."

The boy took the rock and concentrated for a minute before throwing. The stone skimmed the water once and then slipped under the water.

"That wasn't a good one," The little boy said.

"The water's too choppy to get a lot of skips."

"Can I go swimming?"

The father laughed. "It's really cold. Why don't we go back to the hotel and go swimming in the pool?"

The two left hand in hand. The plastic pail barely swinging as it was heavy with pebbles.

Once again the sound of the water hitting the shore was all Laura and Rose could hear. They were alone, but the beach felt crowded. The memories and questions whirled across the sand and the beach grass, all the way down to the water's edge.

"There's something else, isn't there Laura?" Rose asked.

Laura looked at her mother with surprise, but then saddened like she had not been able to hide her feelings from her mother.

"I don't know how to say it," Laura said, shaking her head back and forth. "I don't want to hurt your feelings."

"Tell me," Rose encouraged her. She knew the words she was going to hear would hurt to listen to, but she had to. This was her chance to give Laura what she had deserved but was never able to give her.

"I missed you so much after you died," Laura started to cry. "There were things I wanted to say to you. Things I couldn't discuss with Peter or the kids or friends."

"I heard you every time, Laura," Rose said unequivocally. The truth, Rose reminded herself, was what Laura needed to hear in response, not excuses or blame.

Testing her confidence, Laura pushed on. "I needed your reassurance."

"I know it was hard for you. I'm proud of how well you did. Especially when you persevered and stayed supportive of everyone else when Peter died." The words felt contrived, but they were the only ones that could be used without becoming weapons.

"But I needed you so much," Laura cried desperately through tears. This was not the woman her daughter had become, but the little girl. The little girl she had once been afraid of.

"I've been watching over you all this time, Laura," Rose said firmly without guilt in her voice. Remorse only coated deep in her heart where she hid the feelings.

"I needed you after Little Andrew died. I needed you after Harry was killed," Laura cried, near hysterical. "I was still alive, Mother."

"You had the wisdom and courage to get you through those hard times." Rose's resolve slipped and her lips quivered. "You were stronger than I was."

"Is that your excuse?"

"I'm sorry, Laura," she whispered with the strength she had left and reached out to touch her daughter. Rose watched those pretty eyes, like upside down bowls, spilling tears down her face. "I was there for you as much as I could be. I had to deal with my own pain before I could deal with yours. I was only human. I loved them and I missed them. The same way I loved you and missed you when I died."

"Why did you never tell me? Why did you let me live my life feeling neglected by my own mother?" Laura ranted. "How could you have watched over me? Why didn't I feel you there?"

"I was there. You wanted me there, but you had so much anger with me," Rose accused. "That hurt me too. I was scared of you. You were so pretty like your Grandmother Julia. I didn't think you could love me. She never loved me."

"Look at me," Laura demanded. "I'm not your mother. I was your child. I still am. I needed your love just like you needed hers."

"The things my mother did to hurt me, I know in a way, I turned around and used to hurt you. Anything you did to me, I can't blame you."

"I'm sorry," Laura quieted her voice.

"I forgave you long ago," Rose shook her head back and forth.

The sun began to break through the clouds. Rose noted the position of the sun and stood up, brushing sand off of her skirt. It was time to move on, for both of them.

"Let's go back," Rose beckoned Laura to walk with her.

"I'm confused," Laura said, wiping her face with the backs of her hands. "I feel unhappy and I feel pain. I feel these things and I'm dead."

"Didn't you feel them when you were alive?" Rose asked.

"Yes, but not all the time. I expected it to be gone when I died."

"When you were alive, would you have cherished your happiness as much without the pain?" Rose posed, trying to maintain her balance as she stepped over felled logs while her mind maneuvered amongst the crumbled walls that had kept mother and daughter separated.

"I guess not," Laura said, thoughtfully.

"Don't you expect that your happiness will come from knowing sadness?"

"I don't understand," Laura said, furrowing her brow.

"Sometimes if a soul or spirit isn't prompted by pain or sadness or unhappiness, they cannot make changes for the better," Rose explained. "Even when the person is alive. Don't you think?"

"Perhaps. I guess I have these ideas of what life after death is supposed to be," Laura confessed. "Do you remember my friend Anna? I went to her church with her family a few times and they preached fire and brimstone for all of their sins. You raised us to live by the golden rule, to be honest and respect others and when we die, we would live eternally in the kingdom of Heaven with God and the angels, gold palaces, milk and honey. You wanted us to believe that's where Little Andrew went. Neither one is happening."

Rose acknowledged Laura with a knowing smile. The one thing that remained a constant was Laura's need for her mother and she was thankful. There was so much Rose could still teach Laura. They had both lived full lives of parenting, grand parenting and being wives, but it was reassuring that her daughter still needed her comfort and guidance and she was there to provide it.

"Some have created this ideal about death so they can justify their life. When you die, there are many things you have to take care of. Think of all the questions you had before you died. Did you live with regrets over your lifetime?" Rose asked. "You have to resolve these feelings if you do. Now is the time for you to put your life together the way it needs to be for you to be at peace with it."

The beach was far behind them and the stubby Jack Pine started to grow. The white pine and balsam fir that use to tower over their heads had been pushed back to the ground by the fire decades ago and were now seedlings on their way back to the sky. Rose listened to the fast growing but short lived aspens quake in the breeze.

"You have more questions," Rose stated and turned her attention back to Laura when she noticed her lagging behind.

"You look as old as Grandfather Levi. Little Andrew looks the age that he was when he died. When I first died, I looked like I did when I married Peter. Now I look like I did when my children were little. How is it that I look the age I do?"

"I've come to see that one starts at the age that they encounter their first regrets. The time in their life that they refer back to as a crossroads, a time where they question who they are and what life itself means. As they resolve, answer questions, and discover who they are, they move to the next stage of their heart and outwardly age. Little Andrew is the same age and will stay that way until I leave, as he won't leave until we do. Harry is stuck at his age when Little Andrew died. He has come to little resolve and still blames himself. I worry about him constantly, but there is nothing I can do. This is a journey that Harry must follow to eventually move on."

"How do I resolve these regrets?" Laura said.

"I can't answer that for you. You are the only one with that answer." It had been hard to accept that there was nothing she could have done to save Little Andrew, but more so when she realized her children had to find it within themselves to move on.

"You're supposed to know," Laura glanced at her mother with a slight tease. "You're my mother."

"I'm sorry I don't know." Rose said relieved. The little humor meant her daughter was forgiving her. "Perhaps part of the answer can be found with something simpler. Have you given any thought to who you would like to watch over?"

"Yes. I've decided to watch over Sarah," Laura said confidently.

"Are you sure? Usually your children or another family member is selected."

"Do they have to be? I already consider Sarah family."

"No, they don't have to be," Rose confirmed.

"Then I choose Sarah."

"Why have you decided on her?"

"She needs someone," Laura reasoned and then reconsidered her motives. She still had not been able to recall the question Sarah had asked her back in the nursing home. Laura hoped that part of the memory was tucked away, like a trinket in an unmarked cardboard box, protected but temporarily lost. She dared consider it had ceased to exist when she had died. "Both of my children will be fine. They have each other. Sarah has never had anyone. She was very good at taking care of me when I got sick. Perhaps this is the way I can repay the favor."

"To watch over someone is not a favor. It is done out of love, Laura." Rose said and hoped her daughter realized she had love for her and had just not known how to let it happen.

"I'm not worried about that. I love her."

"You only have one chance to make a change," Rose cautioned.

"I know what I want to do," Laura confided. "I want Sarah to have a baby."

Rose looked at Laura and stopped walking. They were on the way back to the clearing and were on the edge of entering the forest. On the other side of them, the corn had grown tall in the field, but the tassels were still green. Each stalk waved their leaves like careless arms as the hundreds of individual kernels matured, swaddled in the husks. Laura deciding to intervene in Sarah's life with a baby might be possible, but it had its implications.

A baby was a whole new life. Another life was another collection of hopes and dreams. New regrets and new fears.

"Are you sure that's what you want?" Rose asked.

Laura turned around in the middle of the path, realizing her mother had stopped.

"Wouldn't you agree this is a good choice?" Laura asked.

"I'm not saying it is a bad choice. Why do you want to do that?" Rose asked as she approached her daughter. They continued walking, tromping on the thick grass at the edge of the field until they entered the forest where moss lazily covered the ground under the canopy of green leaves.

"I've decided a baby for her would bring her such happiness. This would be Sarah's bridge to having blood kin. This way she would be a part of our family forever."

"Is this the only reason why?" Rose stood in front of her and took both of Laura's hands in hers.

"I would love to have this baby be a reminder that I existed. That I won't be forgotten. I must confess I'm most frightened of being forgotten." Laura stated with deep emotion. "I've wrestled with this for a while. I've looked at my past life experiences. I've pondered what would happen. If I could only go back and do...if I had a chance to do over..." Laura let go of her mother's hands. She became animated with what she was saying by outstretching her hands into the air in effort to make her point. "These are not choices I can make. Nor do I want to change them. I understand I did the best I could. Sarah will die no doubt with questions and issues that she wasn't able to resolve when she was alive. I want the 'what if I had only had a child' not to be one of them."

"You're only lost and forgotten if you lose and forget the importance of family." Rose said with her hands on her hips.

"That may be very true, but I'm also slowly understanding and accepting my place in the family. Between those who are ahead of me and those behind." Laura said expressing her accumulated wisdom to her mother. "I just want Sarah to know that."

"Sometimes Laura," Rose said softly. "The intensity of a person can continue existing without their physical self. Sometimes their significance isn't for the time that they were alive. Sometimes it's after their death," was her final comment.

The breeze high up in the tree tops moved the leaves gently to and fro. The moving shadows cast from the leaves crept across Rose and Laura's faces. The green illumination that created a cool feeling inside of the forest, distorted the color of everything, making it seem surreal. They reached the clearing with both of them looking a little older. They were slowly moving on.

CHAPTER 16

Little Andrew made his way to the beach, as he had so often, looking for Harry. Ordinarily, Little Andrew tagged along with Harry, but his big brother had wandered off without him, which usually meant he was going to the beach. It was funny that Harry seemed to gravitate to this spot, when Little Andrew preferred the farm, especially when his mother had been alive. The house where he had been born and his mother continued to breathe the air in and out. If he could get close enough to her where she could breathe him in, for the moments she held him in her full lungs, he imagined being fully embraced by his mother. But he had been warned about getting too close to the living. He remembered what had happened to Harry when he had been hunting.

When Little Andrew approached, he saw a figure, but it was not Harry. It was Laura. How odd it was to see her in Harry's spot. She just sat there unmoving and staring silently into the distance across the water. He wanted to know why she chose this spot too, so he stayed hidden from sight and watched his big sister through the trees.

The placid surface of the lake was deceiving of its true power that ran in cold currents among the warm water. Little Andrew tried not to look out into the depths of the lake, avoiding the glint of the shiny sun pennies dancing promisingly and so lightly over the deep blue that never seemed to end under frightened feet. His eyes knew the exact spot where he had died and he would experience the nightmare again if he let the sound of the waves crashing to shore fill his ears until all sounds were muffled by tiny bubbles bursting all around him. Fear paralyzed his eyes, remaining free of tears, but they only saw the roiling of water in front of his eyes, watching the air bubbles going up, up where he wanted to go. The last air left his lungs and the water filled them, feeling heavy and pulling him away from the surface where the sun still shone. His nose hurt inside, trying to move the water out and only forcing more in. He coughed and gagged on the water that he had loved to splash Harry and Laura with.

He heard his name, a watery plea that sounded like Harry's voice. Little Andrew tried to reach out to him, but his arms and legs felt too heavy.

And then the water disappeared. He stood on the beach. He watched Harry carrying a body out of the water, limp and dripping which Mother grabbed out of Harry's arms. Sobs shook her frame.

Little Andrew was so bewildered. He felt so neglected that his mother did not comfort him.

"Mother, I'm right here," he cried out, but she ignored him.

"Laura, Harry," Little Andrew ran up to them begging. "I'm right here."

He then realized the body she cradled in her arms was his own. He knew he should feel the hot sand warming his feet, but did not.

Thinking about that day, made him shudder. It was not the drowning or the death that affected him so. It was watching his family load up in the car with his body wrapped in towels and held so tightly by his mother. The car started up and drove away. Little Andrew ran after it.

"Don't leave me, don't leave me, don't leave me," he wailed, until his cries mixed with the dust kicked up by the car. He watched them leave unable to believe he had been left by himself. Mother, Harry, Laura. Not one of them looked back.

With his death, he was so scared, he had to leave everyone who he loved. Grandfather Levi tried to encouraged Little Andrew to go with him. Little Andrew refused. He clung to his family, keeping a wistful eye on them, hanging around the perimeter of the house. He would follow Harry down to the beach where he had drowned. He would dance around Harry, begging him, 'play with me Harry, play with me.' Harry could not hear him.

Little Andrew could hear his mother crying after Harry and Laura left for school in the mornings and his father would be out in the fields working. He would cry out in the yard, 'I'm right here Mother, don't be sad. I'm right here.' The noise coming from him and his mother, the saddest duet. His mother only heard her own sobs.

On the cold November days when the steel grey clouds blotted out the sun, Little Andrew understood, the best of any other time, what loss was. He celebrated his birthday with no cake or presents, but listened to his mother weep. Harry would head to the beach and stare into the lake and when Harry died, Little Andrew would follow a distance behind Harry and wait at the swings at the park that had been built at the beach. Harry would eventually find him there and say it was time to go back.

But that did not fully explain the loss he was feeling. The first cold rain that washed the rest of the fall leaves away from the trees meant the children would not be back to play until spring. Little Andrew would sit in the swing, allowing the wind to push him gently back and forth. His feet barely touched the ground where too many feet to count had carved a bowl shaped depression and when it rained, the water collected into a flat mirror, only reflecting the raindrops that fell on the glassy surface.

The rain streamed down his face as he imagined the happy sounds that came from children playing and the squeaks of the play ground equipment. He loved watching them and tried to pretend he was playing with them.

"Look at me," he would holler. "Look at me." Then his outstretched arms would droop to his sides and the childish grin became a tightened barrier against wordless cries when he realized they couldn't see him.

It was just as well he was at the swings all alone in the park. Sometimes he could feel even more alone when he was surrounded by children when his mind refused to let him pretend he was alive.

He waited patiently for Harry to come get him. Often he would think about what life had been like before he had died. At the age of seven, his curiosity with the world was at its peak. Little Andrew adored his big brother Harry. He loved to play with Harry and Laura. He loved his parents, hoping that life would always be like this, only him growing bigger so he could hunt with Harry and Father and go swimming as far as Harry did. But in his death, Little Andrew was still seven years old and pined for his brother to play with him again.

Then the fateful day when Harry went hunting, Little Andrew had followed. Grandfather Levi had warned him about getting too close to the living. Little Andrew promised himself that he would be careful, he just wanted to be with Harry. It was late morning when another hunter came into the woods and Little Andrew was frightened for

Harry's safety. Harry did not know the other hunter was there. Little Andrew tried to warn him. Only the hunter sensed Little Andrew and thought him a deer. The hunter's rifle barrel followed Little Andrew's presence. The bullets shot past Little Andrew and stopped inside Harry.

Little Andrew had been so scared he would be in trouble. But he was so happy to have Harry join him and keep him company. He had been so lonely with just Grandfather Levi, who he barely remembered when he was alive. Grandmother Julia died, but she left without acknowledging anyone. Then Father. Then Mother. He had not been this happy since the day he drowned in the choppy waters of the lake. Little Andrew would never tell what really had happened to Harry. He would never tell him.

There was still a loss that Little Andrew did not know how to describe. He had Harry. Grandfather Levi. His father saw him from time to time. His mother was now with him and had been for decades. Now Laura had joined them. He should have felt happy, complete. But Mother had been spending a lot of time with Laura. Understandable, but it took time away from him.

Laura still sat on the beach and Little Andrew was getting impatient.

"Laura," he called softly.

An older face of his sister turned to him. Only slight vestiges of the girl he knew when he was alive smiled back at him through the soft folds of wrinkles.

"What are you doing here?" he asked coming out of hiding behind the trees.

"Oh, thinking, I guess."

"What about?"

"My life. The people I loved," she held her hand out to him and he sat down next to her.

Little Andrew thought about what his sister said. "Harry comes here. Do you think he does too?"

He let Laura pull him closer.

"Yes, I'm sure he does."

He waited a moment. "Were you thinking of me?"

"Yes, but I was thinking about Harry too."

"Harry? Why?"

"I'm worried about him."

Little Andrew's lip quivered. For anyone to worry about Harry was reason to cause alarm in his heart.

"Is he okay?"

"I don't know Little Andrew. He needs to move on, but he's afraid."

"He doesn't need to move on. We're all here now," he said defensively.

"You're afraid too."

"He can't leave me."

"No one is going to leave you. If any of us moves on, you will come with us. I promise. You were gone so long, no one is going to leave you," Laura repeated.

Little Andrew was distraught, wanting to believe but unsure. They had all left him once before. He did not want to be forgotten by his brother, but he did not want to hurt Harry either.

"You have to tell him, Little Andrew. The reason he won't move on is because he's afraid to let you down. Tell him if he has to leave you for a while, we won't forget you. We will take care of you."

Little Andrew buried his head in Laura's embrace and hid his tears.

"I can't do it."

"Yes you can. If you really love him, you will."

"Love isn't suppose to hurt, is it?" Little Andrew pulled away from Laura so he could look her in the face.

"Sometimes it does."

"Why?"

"It's hard to explain. Maybe I can show you," she said, caressing his smooth little boy face in her timeworn hands. "Why don't you come with me, I have to go check on Sam and Sarah."

"Can I?" Little Andrew questioned in between sniffs.

"Yes, I would like you to," Laura stood and helped him up. "You'll like Sarah."

Little Andrew quietly followed Laura as they crept around her son's house. In the kitchen they watched Sam chat about his day over dinner while Sarah participated in conversation by periodically peppering Sam's remarks with 'uh-hum' and nodding her head at the appropriate times while absently stabbing at the food on her plate with her fork.

In the coziness of the kitchen with the windows open, allowing the neighborhood noises and scents from other barbeque grills to drift in, Little Andrew thought of eating supper with Laura and Harry, sometimes all of them talking at once. Father might tease or asking questions while Mother seemed to constantly be jumping up to get something or fill an empty spot on someone's plate.

After eating, Sam fell into silence and stared at Sarah. She sat there matching his silence. It was too quiet for Little Andrew. It was the kind of quiet he witnessed after he died when he spied on his family at meal time. After a few minutes Sarah got up to clear the dishes from the table. Sam continued to sit. The dishes clanked together as Sarah stacked them on the counter. The pans banged into each other as they were put into the sink filling with water. A large crash came from the kitchen, followed by smaller pieces hitting the floor.

"Oh damn!" Sarah screamed. "Damn it."

Startled, Little Andrew jumped.

Sam was by her side immediately, leading her from the glass.

"Calm down, honey," Sam commanded as he wrapped his arms around her as if to protect her. "Calm down, it's okay."

Sarah had stopped screaming to start sobbing uncontrollably, gasping for breath. Sam held her that way for several minutes until only the tears flowed down her face. Her body continued to quiver. Little Andrew bit his lip, trying not to cry too.

"Tell me what's going on, honey," Sam pleaded.

"I...I don't know what to think," Sarah whispered through the sobs. "The doctor called and told me about the test results today."

Little Andrew looked up at Laura, wondering what kind of tests a doctor would give a person. Sarah could not possibly be this upset about math problems or spelling.

"What did he say?" Sam asked, gravely.

"The tests were inconclusive. There's no reason why we can't have a baby, but we aren't," She sniffed.

'The baby,' Little Andrew remembered.

"We will Sarah, we will."

"But Sam, it's been years." She said, irritated. "I'm tired of taking care of other people's children. I'm tired of loving other people's children. Can't you understand that?"

Little Andrew could only imagine what kind of children she took care of. He pictured Sarah hugging sad children while she rocked them back and forth. Other children probably stood around her, waiting their turn. He imagined himself waiting for her comfort.

"You have to be patient," he tried to reason. "We have to be patient."

Sarah sighed abruptly and released herself from his embrace.

"I want to know now. I want to know what it feels like, inside to feel alive. I feel dead. Right here," she yelled and beat her chest with her fists over her heart. "You don't understand, Sam. I'm not happy with my life. My empty life. My life with no family. You don't know what that feels like."

Little Andrew squeezed Laura's hand. He knew all too well what Sarah was saying. He had not felt alive for years and years. Empty was a good way to explain it.

"Sarah," Sam started sternly. "When you married me, you got a family."

'We are family,' Little Andrew said proudly, in his head.

"It's so easy for you to say that," Sarah said flatly. "You've always had a family."

She left the room and cried her way upstairs to the bedroom. She lay on the bed sobbing while Little Andrew and Laura stood by the window in the hall and watched her. He wondered if Sarah felt the despair he had once felt as he watched his family drive away from the beach and left him, mourning over a body that was no longer alive.

They could hear Sam cleaning up the broken dish downstairs before he joined Sarah in the bedroom. He gently stroked her hair as tears streamed down her face. Little Andrew wished he could do this for his mother when she had cried when she was alive.

"It's okay, it's okay. We will have a baby." Sam gently whispered. Sarah continued to cry.

Little Andrew watched his sister listening intently outside the doorway in the shadows. The light on the night stand spilled yellow into the hallway. Sam and Sarah couldn't see them, but they still stood on the other side where the darkness held its own against the light.

"If we don't have one ourselves we might look at adopting."

Sarah turned over and faced Sam. "Baby," She started as she touched his face. "You are so sweet, that might work if it comes to that."

Sam looked questioningly at her. "Are you saying that's not what you want?"

Sarah sighed. "How do I explain it to you? It's more than hearing someone calling me mommy. It's not completely that I want a baby but I want a part of you also. I want to watch our child grow, watch a reflection of the beauty I see in you."

"Honey, you are so beautiful, I can only imagine the joy of watching our baby grow."

"On another level," Sarah expressed. "I want to know what it feels like..."

Sam smiled at Sarah. "To give birth?"

Sarah looked away from him and did not respond right away. "What it feels like to know someone that I'm related to, that I'm a part of." Sarah looked back into his eyes. "To feel a part of something, to belong."

"Tell me more. I want to understand how you feel."

"Our baby would mean I'm legitimately part of your family. I would fit in then. I would feel like I fit in. I'm ready to become that person, even if it means leaving a part of me behind."

"What would you be leaving behind?"

Sarah bit her lip, knowing she had said too much.

Sam held her in his arms. "You, Sarah, are a part of me, part of my life, part of my family. If a baby is what you need, I will do everything I can to make it happen." He held up her left hand and fingered her wedding band.

"I know you want a baby," Sam confirmed.

"It's more than a baby. I want to watch it grow up and learn to walk and talk and run and play on the swings. I want to watch him grow into an adult and experience the world and have babies of his own," Sarah said softly. "I grew up and there was no one to watch and love me and praise me and be proud of me. I really want that."

Little Andrew never knew someone alive could feel the way he had. Before Harry had joined him, he felt like there was no one to watch over and love him. He had constantly feared he would be alone again if separated too long from Harry and be forgotten. But Sarah's words made him realize he would never grow up and forever be a little boy, forever in eternity and that made him sad. He would never get older like others who lived beyond seven years old. He died at the age of seven and would be forever remembered at that age and never thought of as older with wrinkles or white hair. Little Andrew would never grow to be a man. He would never know the pain of life, nor the joy of being an adult.

"I never grew up," he whispered out loud. "I'll never be anything except a child." Laura's arms tightened around him, trying to comfort him. All of the fears and anxieties seemed to hover momentarily, quivering in a stationary spot while Little Andrew saw clearly what his loss was. It was not Harry or Mother or someone else he missed. It was himself that never was, the adult he would never be.

CHAPTER 17

On the path near the creek that meandered through the forest, the brush was very thin along the banks as the forest animals, particularly the deer, had created trails, packing the earth hard, along this body of water. In the bed of the creek, patches of stagnant puddles stood waiting for a summer rain to allow them to flow again, as it was reaching the end of summer. The low buzz of mosquitoes gave sound to the air heavy from the humidity. Levi was making his way to the top of the hill with his granddaughter following behind.

Laura's presence had stirred pangs for his wife Julia. He marveled at how much Laura looked like his beloved Julia. But Laura radiated more beauty than his wife ever had. The willingness to accept the life she had been given and not blame others for the life she did not have was something Julia had never been capable of. Watching Laura, Levi realized how Julia's beauty had been veiled with unhappiness and regrets. She had cloaked herself with the dreams of New York she wanted so badly, like a fabric so showy and gaudy, yet unable to insulate her from the cold reality of frontier life.

It seemed a lifetime of standing in a bitter rain for Levi while Julia's glare showered him with animosity. There was always the unspoken accusation he stood between her and New York. He felt her coldness taunting him, belittling him for what he was not able to provide her with. Despite the insinuations of their relationship, he had no other choice, he loved her. Afraid of where Julia's jealousies might lead her, he distributed his affections carefully with their daughters, Rose and Lily. Even with their daughters, he was afraid she might see it as him being unfaithful to her.

Levi only became more committed and believed he could save her from despair if he could give her infinite amounts of love when Lily died. He gave to his wife unwittingly and watched helplessly as Julia took Lily's death out on Rose. It pained him to see her torment Rose, but he was so sure Julia would see him as being disloyal to her if he comforted the daughter who broke the doll. He knew it was just a doll, not the flesh and blood and feelings and a heart able to break as with Rose. But that doll meant more to Julia than her own daughter. After the day the doll was broken, Julia changed. More so, it seemed, than when Lily died. But she had already spent so much time grieving, the loss very real and important to Julia regarding that china doll.

For him to intervene would cause Julia to release untold retribution, but worse yet, he knew it would be their daughter, who was still alive, who would suffer the most. Despite this, Rose grew into a strong woman, stronger than her mother ever could be. Only recently could he admit, stronger than he too, and was grateful to have watched Rose be a devoted wife and attentive mother to Harry, Laura, and Little Andrew. While everyone knew of her husband's unfaithfulness, she acted like it was not happening, determined to not take anyone's pity. Levi was relieved when Rose joined him when she died and thankful that she would accept his love he had been unable to give during their lifetime. It was like she understood his weaknesses and forgave him.

It did not matter how much Laura reminded him of Julia. He had to learn to love others. He would not fall victim again to the empty promises he had created in hopes of obtaining Julia's false love.

"What does this all mean?" Laura asked as she stopped short of the creek where the path crossed.

"What are you referring to Laura?" he replied.

"I would have thought the purpose of life would have been clear after I had died," she said, grabbing a branch that was in her way.

"Because you didn't figure it out when you were alive?" Levi stopped at a fallen log and carefully sat down on it.

"When I was alive, I did my best as a wife and mother. Sometimes I was better at it than other times," Laura admitted. "I tried to be a good person to others, but still, I'm not sure if I lived a good life."

"Wouldn't you consider that a successful life? Doing your best?"

"That's easy to agree with in words," she sighed and turned her head to look at the valley below them, resting her hands on her hips. "To live it though, it's not so simple to determine."

Levi lit his pipe and puffed on it to get it started. The smoky sweet smell kindled while he sought out glimpses of the landscape through the patchy parts of the brush. When he was alive, he had planted an apple orchard on this side of the hill. Nestled with neighboring hills, it effectively cupped itself around the valley. It was not until he died and Julia sold the farm did he realize how much he loved the delicate spring bloom of the trees and the bees swarming the petals. Love seemed to blossom with things he could not have.

From atop the hill, he longed to share with his granddaughter, this vista of delicate veils hung from the branches of the fruit trees. He liked to watch the workers, like the bees, scurry around the trees the rest of the time. Winter they pruned the branches and suckers, leaving a bare minimum of branches so it still resembled a tree and in the summer the grass was mowed underneath the shade and the tops of the trees sprayed. By the fall, the hard green fruit had swelled into rosy skinned sweetness and was picked one by one to be placed in the baskets strapped to the worker's bodies. One could believe they had found the answer to life watching the bees, so happily engrossed in the bliss of a blossom, buried deep with the pollen dust coating them as they sucked up the elixant nectar.

"Being the best person you can be is only a small part of understanding," he said and stroked his beard. "Forgiving is another part. For example your Grandmother Julia has spent the last fifty years walking the streets of New York trying to find the family fortune. She's trying to find the happiness that she once had there. She has been unable to forgive and forget. Even in death. She cannot forgive those who wronged her nor can she forgive herself."

"Grandmother Julia," Laura mused. "Sarah had been trying to find her for so long. While I was alive, I wasn't able to help her with names, dates or places to find her. Perhaps I can guide her to find Julia as I watch over her."

"Sarah may be looking for Julia in the past, but you have to remember that families grow forwards as well as backwards. You know you only have one chance to intercede, whether it is planned out or saved for an emergency. Think very hard before you decide, because you will be deciding for her also."

"Is it hard for you to be without Grandmother Julia?" Laura asked.

He thought for a moment, deciding how to word his answer. It was more complicated than being without the woman he loved. Julia was so precious to him. He loved the contrast of her beauty against the ruggedness of the wilderness. Her refinement and grace seemed to dance above the rough and hard and calloused dispositions of the other women who had made the northern woodlands their home. He would never tell her this, knowing she would have been insulted, as if he were mocking her sophistication, cheapening it by comparing it against the savage living that seemed to be required.

When Julia came to him and told him she was ready to marry him, Levi for the first time saw her vulnerabilities. He promised himself he would screen them from the rest of the world seeing them, as he knew others could be cruel and take advantage of her. He already knew the rumors of why her family fled to Michigan. What Julia's family did not say and what Julia professed, Levi found the truth in the stories. The beliefs Julia had about the truths and the lies would crush her already fragile spirit if she knew what he had figured out. Her father had drank and gambled what money they had acquired. The money her mother hid, ran out shortly after they arrived in Michigan. Julia's mother had confided in the storekeeper and given him the rest of the money she had. She said under no circumstances should her husband know about the money. It was to be used by her to purchase food. The secret she begged him to keep circulated through the town, but managed not to reach her or her daughter's ears in return.

He had never doubted he was not good enough for Julia. He pursued her and her sadness, knowing he wanted to make her happy. It wasn't her beauty he wanted to own, but to protect. He wanted to protect her and give her everything he was capable of. It was selfishness knowing that everything he could give her was not even close to what he wanted to give her. It was so much more that she deserved, so what he did have, he gave to Julia in abundance.

There was a sharpness to her exterior. To others it was perceived to be veneered in meanness, when she was only trying to cover up her vulnerabilities. Levi never dared to determine if it was sheer ignorance or self defense that she seemed unaware of how everyone else saw her as or the rest of her family as. And it was her family who had left her powerless, equipping her with tools meant for refined society, not the frontier life required in a state whose drawn boundary lines were not much older than she. Because she had been unable to have any say in the move to Michigan, she had to feel in control, even though on her own, she would have been helpless to take care of herself. But his infinite love had not been enough for Julia to find peace. As Julia got older, he regretted never taking her back to

New York. He knew he gave Julia's guilt trips life when he kept this regret in his heart, even in death.

"I loved Julia more than she would ever understand. I knew Julia more than she would ever realize. I don't know why, I just thought if I loved her enough, she might be happy. But she never was because I could never give her what she wanted."

"I think a lot of people fell short of that."

"She became increasingly bitter as she lived her last years. It was like she knew that going back to New York would never happen when she became so old. She was angry because she felt her life had not been her own. The decisions that were made for her life had been dictated by the wants and needs of her parents and then her own family with me. Your Grandmother Julia never resolved moving from New York. If Julia isn't able to resolve all of the conflicts in her life, it will guarantee her an unhappy and unfulfilled eternity. After she died, I tried to convince her come back from New York. She doesn't belong there but she wouldn't listen. She just won't believe it. It wasn't until I realized I had no control over her ability to forgive, could I move on."

"She had to be miserable to have lived so bitterly," Laura deduced with melancholy. "She never knew the love that surrounded her."

"She wasn't the only one who didn't know what love really was. I loved your Grandmother Julia so much, I didn't think I could spare any to give to anyone else. For her, what I gave to her, I couldn't give to my daughters. They needed me too, but I was selfish and gave everything to Julia, thinking she would love me back."

"But love can be infinite. Before Sam was born I was scared I wouldn't be able to love him like I loved Karen. I was surprised that I had more and more, I didn't need to divide my love between them."

"One has to believe it's infinite, not afraid of it running out. It's taken me a long time to figure it out."

"How come you're still here then?" Laura asked.

He smiled as if he had been had. "I guess I must learn to love those I didn't while I was alive."

"And when you have?"

"I will make sure my grandchildren's children know they can love more than one person. They have to love more than one person. People can stop loving you, but you should have others to fill that void. If you love only one person who never loves you back, you have nothing."

"How long does this take? How long before you can move on?"

"It takes as long as it needs too, my dear," He cleared his throat. "I have work to do still, watching over my children's children and their babies. In a way as I watch them grow and enter new life stages, I'm not absolved for not caring for my loved ones like I should have when I was alive, but I am forgiven. I was human, not perfect."

"If only Grandmother Julia could say that," Laura commented.

"I don't know if she ever will. She has forgotten the family she created in her search for the one she came from."

"I'm afraid of being forgotten," she said quietly.

"Most everyone feels that way. You can forever contemplate being forgotten or resolve that your love and care is enough to make your mark on your family and loved ones. You will never be forgotten. Without you, your children wouldn't exist and your grandchildren wouldn't exist and so on."

"But people seem to disappear without traces of their lives or daily contributions to their families or the places they lived."

"Some of the lucky ones continue their existence postmortem through stories about them or exaggerated tales handed down to the next generation," he offered.

"What about those that don't have children?" Laura asked, thinking of Sarah.

Levi smiled. "They touch the lives of the people around them. They can change the life of another person for the better and unfortunately, sometimes not in a good way. They can then spend a lot of time after death contemplating their choices and deciding if they are willing to make peace with themselves."

"Grandmother Julia is still going through that struggle," Laura said.

"Julia will be found again and remembered, I know she will." Levi said in a tone that sounded like he knew more than he was saying. "Some find so much enjoyment or meaning from earthly things. Where I am now, I see this as too present minded of the living. If the earth was intended for mortals, finding infinite comfort and enjoyment from it would be logical. But remember, mortal means death. There's much more importance in the definition on the dead than the living."

"I'm sure this is an answer to one of my questions, but I don't quite know what I should be asking."

"Basically, Laura, living is where all the mistakes are made. Death resolves them." Levi tapped the ashes out of his pipe. "For some people the fear of dying is so scary that they deny its reality. They think they will somehow continue living until they can sort out and deal with the realities of death. They're afraid of death. They're afraid of the unknown. They envision things so bad that any good is not worth the risk of finding out. Others spend their time and energy looking for a cure for death. They just know something could work, but they are too scared to deal with their own eminent end to life. They are consumed with perpetuating their life, rather than making peace with death."

"Do some really believe that they can keep living beyond the odds? For what? For further accomplishment?" Laura asked.

"I guess. Death is something rarely embraced. If someone does, everyone around them wants to know what their problem is. Why wouldn't they want to stay alive? There's the contradiction. A better place in death, but yet no one is eager to get there," Levi informed her. "Yet, others are so bitter with life and harbor such intense hatred they do not want to be remembered. They are the saddest. They are likely to never resolve the pain and injustices they felt in life. They don't move on because they are afraid of the unknown. They're afraid of being wrong. Afraid to see their real self, they might not even know who that is. You, Laura, might help someone like Sarah to not suffer this, but you may also be able to help those that are already dead and don't know how to move on. Everyone has to realize that life requires a lot of forgiveness."

Levi finished speaking and stood up to stretch. He glanced at Laura and her face looked like she still had questions. "Tell me what you're thinking," he invited.

She set her shoulders straight, bracing herself with courage before she spoke. "Do you have memories that you have forgotten? Parts of memories?"

"What do you mean?"

"I," Laura stammered, like she was afraid to explain. "I don't know. I have all these memories and I don't know what I'm supposed to do with them. Then there are memories I know I've forgotten and if I could only remember them, I think I would know." She stood, ready to follow him down the crest of the hill.

"A river is different than a lake or an ocean," he gestured with his hand toward the dry creek. "Even the slowest of flows has an ever changing quality. Watch a leaf fall to the surface of the river. It's constantly rushing to a new and changing destination but it will take that leaf with the currents. At the lake or the ocean, that same leaf would only ride the waves with the wind pushing at its backside. It doesn't have a destination like the water that flows along the river banks."

She stopped walking and looked at him with confusion on her face.

"Don't worry about your destination, Laura. Your journey isn't over for much longer." He grasped her hand, hoping she understood what he was trying to share with her.

Trying to love Julia, giving it to her exclusively, he had lost so much by not sharing. He realized this only when he could not convince her to come back to Michigan and conceded his love would never be accepted by her. He had loved the wrong things. By sharing what he loved rather than loving who he could not have, he might be vindicated.

Resolving to leave Julia to memory he was able to shed his selfish ways and he could show

Laura the pieces, what he understood about life and by holding them up next to each other she might see where they fit. He was confident Laura would figure it out and she would not be forgotten.

CHAPTER 18

New York was the center of the world for Julia, where she was born and spent her childhood. It was apparent at an early age Julia would become a woman of intense beauty. Her straight Roman nose, exuding power, was flanked by green eyes, recalling the lushness of the Scottish highlands. It was the kind of beauty that would be rewarded when draped with richly dyed silks against her pale milky skin. Her cheeks blushed to the color of apple blossoms, radiated from the blood circulating shallowly beneath the buttery texture of her skin. The whiteness of her teeth, uncommon in a world of tea stains and decay, flashed in a frame of full rose petal pink lips when she smiled.

She could play princess if she wanted, even though she was already from a family of high society. Jewels, horses, dresses and an elegant home. Her family surrounded her with refinement and things of beauty. For her seventh birthday she received a beautiful china doll from her parents. She had come all the way from France and held the allure of a faraway place of castles and kings and queens with her porcelain head and hands and the shinny pink taffeta dress trimmed with lace.

Julia remembered that this was a happy time with her parents. The arguments had subsided between Mother and Father and there was money to spoil Julia with gifts. The happy time was only that, as it lasted only a few years. But the arguments between her parents increased again. Mother would accuse her father of trying to ruin their family. Then one day, Aunt Hazel came to the house and started helping Mother pack. Julia hid behind corners and listened in on their conversations. She heard Mother tell Aunt Hazel that Father had gambled the house. Father had ruined them. They were going to have to start over in a new place. Thank goodness she had hid money from him. Father had the good fortune to find work with the railroad in northern Michigan, through connections here in the East.

Mother stuffed as many of Julia's pretty dresses into satchels. Julia was allowed to take her china doll from France, if she could carry it because there would be no other room on the journey to Michigan. They left the maid and houseboy, and the furniture at the house in New York. Julia questioned how they would live without these things. Her mother said they had to be sold. They would get what they needed when they got to their new home.

The house they were to live in at Michigan was newly built, but had been constructed quickly and the rough sawn boards let cold drafts blow through. "We're lucky to have it," her mother could be heard mumbling. "Only through providence, we're not homeless." Sleeping on blankets on the floor eventually became straw mattresses on the floor. A table and assortment of chairs came to them in just barely usable shape. None had the pretty turning or rich tapestry seats. It was now Mother's responsibility to run the household and do the cooking.

Julia felt cold and tired all the time from the work her mother instructed her to do. One cold morning, her mother asked her to pump water. With a rumbling stomach, hungry for breakfast, Julia refused, stating that was servants work. Julia's cheek burned with her mother's hand informing her that she was no longer a child of privilege. The thought fell heavily into her mind with tears spilling out of her eyes, but she did not dare ask Mother were the hidden money was and why they did not use it.

In the wilds of northern Michigan, Julia would play with her doll, twirling her so the full skirts would billow out with a swishing sound and pretend they were still in New York. She remembered the balls her parents would hold where all the ladies were dressed so pretty and sparkled with jewels and the men looked so handsome dressed in black and white. They arrived in fancy carriages pulled by beautiful horses, neighing among the greetings and music filling the air. As she grew older she would believe she would go back to New York and dance at the fancy parties.

Sitting on the bed, she would rub the doll's dress between her fingers, forgetting the dress she wore had a tear in the elbow where it had worn so thin.

Julia grew into the beautiful young lady everyone expected. She wanted to go out East, have pretty dresses and hats made for her to wear. She proposed that she could stay with Aunt Hazel, go to parties and meet the young wealthy men. Her mother forbade it, telling her this was where she belonged. Ruefully, Julia felt her mother was ashamed of what they had become in the woods of Northern Michigan, where refinement only came in crates shipped from New York.

The single men Julia's age were met with icy looks cascading down from the slope of her nose. One man was not deterred and would compliment her whenever he passed her on the way to the shop or to church. He eventually got Julia to laugh, to shed the haughty cloak of refinement. She told him no, over and over, that she did not want to marry him. Julia did not intend to hurt Levi's feelings by telling him no a second time. He would not understand how if she agreed to marry him, returning to New York would become less and less of a possibility. That was not entirely true. Levi had told her, if she wanted to visit New York, they could, but to live there, he was not sure of.

"I remember New York too, and there were too many people there for me," Levi had told her. "I want to farm here. I want the forests and the lakes surrounding me."

"It's so uncivilized here sometimes," Julia tried to convince him.

What she could not say is, if she married him and went to New York, no other man could take her and give her the life she pined for. The only men who could do that were already living in New York, far from where she was and where she could not catch any of their eyes. Levi was so good to her, he made her laugh, but she clung to her dream of returning to New York, the only place she knew she would be happy. She spent weeks reassuring herself she had done the right thing by telling Levi no again when she spied him taking another girl home from church. It was that homely Maude and Julia would not stand for being replaced by her. Jealousy urged her to take back what she had been given before she had nothing.

"You want to marry me?" Levi asked seriously and stroked his beard thoughtfully while looking into Julia's beautiful face.

"Yes, if you'll only ask me again," she told him in the softest voice she knew.

"That will be the third time," he pulled her close to kiss her. "You wouldn't break my heart a third time, would you?"

"Only if you don't ask," Julia knew she had him.

"But I need to ask you one thing," he whispered into her ear, his whiskers tickling the nape of her neck. "Will you be my wife here, in Michigan?"

Julia hesitated. Either answer, she would have to give something up. She could have Levi and the hope of returning to New York and going to parties and the theater. And maybe finding the money she remembered overhearing her mother say she hid. Then she could buy the furs and the jewels and the pretty dresses she remembered. Then a fleeting thought of becoming a spinster in the wilds of Michigan shot through her.

"Yes, I will be your wife here." She said and then felt him wrap his arms around her so tightly she could barely breathe. He truly loved her and she could learn to love him back, in time, she thought.

Despite her promises to Levi, Julia begged to move back to New York, trying to romanticize what their life would be like there. But then the first baby came and it squashed her dreams of living in New York again. Baby Rose was nothing to show off, with her wide set brown eyes, nose with a bump in it and thin lips. Then came Baby Lily. She was a beautiful baby in all respects. Julia knew she had become too old to be one of the refined young ladies from out East. The embers of her dreams died like pieces of spent charcoal, but the birth of Lily ignited hope that she might have a chance of becoming part of high society again.

All too soon, Julia's hopes ended with Lily's death. She resigned a little to the fact her home was the wilderness, but held fast to the constant memories of her childhood home.

Julia watched her other daughter Rose grow up and marry. Rose seemed to be content with life where it was. But Rose had never known any other place. Her head had not been filled with stories of New York, like she had placed in Lily's ears as if they were precious little jewels to secret away. Julia's pride was rekindled again when Rose gave birth to a daughter who reclaimed the family's beauty. That daughter was Laura, the spitting image of her beautiful grandmother.

On the busy streets, horns honked and engines roared, creating a din of too many sounds, none truly decipherable. This was New York. The city that sometimes is referred to without being called a city. A woman in her early twenties paced back and forth along the crowded sidewalk. She wore a dress of rich brocade and a large velvet skirt that reached the ground. Her hair, braided and coiled under the brim of her hat, contrasted with the modern apparel worn by the throngs of people passing by. It was very stylish for a well to do lady of the time. Now, her dress and hat was faded and dusty from decades of wear.

Julia hesitantly walked among the crowded sidewalks. She tried to stay out of people's ways, but it was impossible to do with so many people hurrying along. It was uncomfortable to have someone walk through her, and it left the person with a chill.

There was such a diversity in the skin colors of the people, their clothes, the way the wore their hair, and the way they smelled. But Julia was looking for something specific. She was looking for her parents or the money, any clues that might lead her to them.

Over a hundred years ago there was a two-story house with a fence around it. Colossal buildings reaching to the sky, hundreds of stories high, now stood in that spot. The big oak trees that shaded the house in the summer were now replaced with skyscrapers that never let the sun shine down to the hard, hard pavement. Also gone, were the rolling hills of soft grasses that lent themselves to mid afternoon naps and daydreams. This had been Julia's world when she was a child. Her father's job was with the railroad. Her mother's job was to oversee the house and servants. The servant's job was to help clean the house, fix the meals, and work in the garden. Julia's job was to play with her doll.

At one time this was considered the country. Julia's family had a house in the city also. The countryside disappeared as it became absorbed by the growing city, tenfold, as the wave of the city's growth pushed outward in all directions.

Back then, the city also meant parties. Her parents were hosts and guests of some of the most lavish parties. At the country house during the summer, Julia would dance among the tall grasses. High up in the trees she would peek through the branches and pretend she was sneaking a look at the fancy parties through the banister rail at the city house. In the fall she would use acorn caps as fragile stemware to hold her wine.

This was all gone. The parties, the little acorns, the waving grasses were buried under the concrete monolith of the city. The house was gone, her parents disappeared and the money lost. The only thing still present were Julia's memories, if she only could let herself fall into their reality, but the abyss between her and the past was too great.

Julia tirelessly hoped to recognize her parents, Aunt Hazel or anyone who might help her find the money. She looked into all the faces that passed her. She recognized no one and none of them even looked at her. Occasionally one of the dead would stop, relief relaxing their shoulders and anticipating Julia was who they were looking for. But they always moved on, they were looking for someone or something else too.

"Julia?" a woman asked, startling Julia from her thoughts. "Grandmother Julia?"

"Yes?" Julia said as she recognized the features of the woman's face, but was not sure who this was.

"I'm Laura, your grandchild," Laura hesitated. "My mother, Rose, is your daughter. Do you remember? I don't think you ever saw me this old."

"Oh, child," Julia said, as her face softened with a smile. The only thing Rose had done well was giving birth to that beautiful girl Laura. "Are you with us now?"

"Yes Grandmother Julia, I am."

"Have you come to look for the family's money with me?"

"No, I have not." Laura said sadly.

"Oh," Julia said, forlorn. "Why have you come?"

"I want you to come back with me," Laura smiled and took her grandmother's hands in hers. "To Michigan to be with your husband and your children and your grandchildren."

Julia looked down the street with sad eyes. It was alive and moving. Only Julia stood as still as the buildings.

"This is where I belong," she proclaimed.

"Are your parents here?" Laura inquired. "Do you have family here with you?"

"I don't know where my family is. I assume they went back to Ireland. I don't know where they went, so I can't find them," Julia said, gazing across the street, but really looking at nothing. Her heart burned, not wanting to believe her family had abandoned her. Even in death.

"Why are you staying here alone?" Laura asked. "Come back with me."

"I have to stay here," Julia said, with determination. "I was happy here. This is the closest I can be to happiness."

"Grandfather misses you. Mama misses you. Harry and Little Andrew miss you," Laura pleaded. "I miss you."

The memory of how Levi had come for her burned in her throat, sharp and acidic.

"Rose is dying," Levi had told her. "This is your chance to make up to her."

"For what?" Julia said haughtily

"You hurt her, Julia."

'Her scars were all self-inflicted."

"She needs you."

"Everyone dies. People have been dying for thousands of years. No one was there for me."

"I was," Levi tried to sound convincing. "Come back, my dear. You are as fragile and broken as your doll."

How dare he mock her like that. Whatever guilt she had for Rose was extinguished by the memory of her daughter breaking her prized possession.

"The money was taken away from me. Lily was taken away from me. Now you want to take my last chance to find everything away from me?"

"This isn't your home. It never was. You died the day you left New York, because you refused to live in the present. You never knew what it was like to be alive. You refused to be a daughter, a wife, a mother."

Julia stayed silent, still refusing to tell Levi how she felt. Eyes brimming, she felt disheartened that no one, her parents or Levi, had ever been there for her. Everyone just wanting from her for their own needs. "You only gave me empty promises," she choked on tears as she told him.

"You don't understand," Julia tried to explain to Laura, as exasperation crept into her tone. "This is where our family is supposed to be, but they have forgotten me."

"No one has forgotten you." Laura tried to convince. "You would know that you are not forgotten if you would come back. Come back and see my son and daughter, your great, great grandchildren."

"If they were patient, they would be able to find the money with me."

"Can't you let it go?" Laura asked angrily. "You would be very rich if you could see how much you are loved."

"I was happy here..." Julia had started walking again as she felt the sadness creep into every corner of her soul. She left Laura standing there as she drifted down the street in the foot traffic.

CHAPTER 19

Laura entered the forest clearing where buckthorn and wild grape vine forcefully dominated the copse edges. Her melancholy lifted upwards toward the sky like the stately pines, swaying back and forth in the breeze as if they rocked babies in their boughs. She was disappointed Grandmother Julia had not come with her. On her way back to Michigan, she thought about Grandfather Levi's words again. More and more of it was making sense and she pondered what else she could learn. Perhaps, if she listened hard enough, more answers about life would be unveiled. But learning the truth was sometimes uncomfortable.

How painful it had been to learn her mother had been so frightened of her beauty she had inherited from Grandmother Julia. From the daguerreotypes of her mother, Laura knew her mother had grown up as a plain child compared to her sister, Lily, or her mother, Julia. Laura considered her mother knew all too well a beautiful shell, empty inside, lost its appeal after time. Her mother's goal had been to raise Laura to learn humility and compassion, knowing her true beauty would then be seen. Her mother had apologized for her neglect, but Laura had yet to accept her forgiveness completely. Laura's anger at her mother had slowly turned to guilt and shame. She had craved her mother's attention and now she felt like she had behaved like a selfish child. Laura wanted to bask in delight, seeing her mother proud of her. It was a feeling she had been longing for from her mother for years. Slowly her animosity towards her mother was evolving into compassion and understanding.

Her heart was heavy, but she felt energized with purpose. In the clearing Laura found Harry sitting on the ground with his back against a log. She now looked old enough to be his mother. She had aged outwardly after visiting Julia in New York. Harry continued to look like he did at nineteen. His youthful looks reminded that his life had held so much promise.

"Where have you been?"Harry looked up and asked.

"I went to find Grandmother Julia so I could talk to her."

"In New York?"

"Yes." She said and sat down next to him.

"How was she?"

"I'm not sure how to describe it. When I left here, I had hopes that I could convince her to come back home. She has no family out there. She's alone.

I was still hopeful at that point. But she's very adamant that she must find the family's money."

"So it's true? She's still looking for the money."

"It's sad Harry. It's apparent Grandmother Julia is lost because she doesn't know where she needs to be. She won't move on."

Harry did not respond. Laura was not sure if she had struck a nerve with Harry or if he was waiting for her to go on. She decided to continue, but with the intention of getting him to open up.

"This is so different," Laura uttered.

"What do you mean?"

"I never would have dreamed that this is what it would be like after I died."

"I don't think anyone does."

"What do you think about all of this?" she asked him.

"It's odd," Harry said. "I'm getting some satisfaction now that I never did while I was alive."

"You mean taking care of Little Andrew?" she said carefully.

Harry set his jaw and looked down at his hands.

"I'm sorry. I didn't mean to hurt you," she laid her hand on his.

"It's true, I guess," He answered. "I failed miserably when I was alive. No one blames me, but I still feel guilty. It feels like it wouldn't be any worse had I taken his life with my own hands."

"Don't say that, Harry." She shook her head in disbelief.

"But I can't deny my feelings," he protested.

Laura nodded in agreement.

"There were a few women who I had courted. Early on they made it clear to me they were looking for someone to take care of them. That frightened me. How could I take care of someone who I love if I had failed so miserably with Little Andrew?"

"You take it so personal. Don't you think Mother and Father have felt the same way? Who's to blame? It happened. It's very sad, but none of us ended up saving him."

Laura could not recall ever seeing Harry cry. Now his tears held pain that compared to no other sadness. He had taken this anguish to the grave and it followed him into death with greater enormity then could be imagined.

"After I died," Harry said, as he wiped his face dry with a handkerchief. "It was almost a relief and honor to watch over Little Andrew until Mother joined us."

"But Harry," Laura questioned. "Isn't it the living we're supposed to watch over?"

"Don't you think Little Andrew is deserving?" he asked defensively.

"I'm not saying that. What I'm saying is Little Andrew is dead." She wrapped an arm around his shoulders. In hushed tones she continued. "Grandmother Julia won't move on. She lived her life in the past, always yearning for New York. She continues to live in that past."

Laura moved away from Harry a little so she could look him in the eyes as she spoke. "Harry, she won't let go. She's doomed for an eternity of sadness and regret. She's the only one who can change it."

Harry refused to look at her and crossed his arms, braced with silence. It frustrated her that he would not listen. It had to be hard for him to take her seriously when he most likely still considered her a little sister. She understood the smothering feeling he must have been feeling with her trying to mother him. He had to feel uncomfortable with their roles reversed, like Karen had done to her. Laura had fought it and now Harry was refusing to hear anything she said that might have a ring of truth because it felt like failure to admit defeat.

"You need to let go Harry. You need to forgive yourself. By blaming yourself you are only hurting Little Andrew. You need to move on so Little Andrew may move on too."

Harry looked miserable. Laura knew that even giving up his unhappiness would be difficult. Changing would require Harry to step into the unknown. Most of a lifetime and all of his years in death he had lived in guilt, all other things were forgotten. This was all he knew.

"If nothing else, do it for Little Andrew. Laura pleaded. Save him from an eternity like Grandmother's."

Laura knew that Harry understood the importance of family, but he did not know the forgiveness his family had for him. He knew how to forgive others, yet he did not know how to forgive himself. How far could she push him, she tried to guess. As much as needed, if it made him act, but there was a risk it would drive him away.

"I never felt it was your fault Harry, but you need to hear this. I forgive you for not saving Little Andrew. That was not your chance to intercede when Little Andrew died. Your chance to intercede is now. But you can't until you forgive yourself. You're almost as bad as Grandmother Julia. Look around and see who needs you now."

"It's not that easy," he said, angrily.

"You're right. If you keep your head bowed in guilt for eternity, you'll never know."

"Have you decided for yourself who you are going to help?" Harry taunted.

Laura was thoughtful. "Yes. I'm going to help Sarah," was her answer.

"It's been so easy for you," Harry said in an accusatory tone. "You've got it all figured out."

"You're just afraid of being told you're wrong," Laura matched his impudence. "You don't know what it's like to be alive. Since the day Little Andrew died, you've been dead. Just going through the motions of being alive. Your guilt has been your obsession. You need to forgive yourself and let Little Andrew go. He only stays because he wants to please you."

"It's more than that."

"You're afraid, Harry. You're afraid of what might happen if you did forgive yourself. At least do it and teach Little Andrew what it is to forgive one's self. Don't count on him freeing himself of his own regrets."

Laura accepted Harry glaring at her. She had spoken words that needed to be said and no one had been brave enough to hurt him so he could free himself of the prison of guilt he had created. It was up to him to internalize the decision to move on. Too easily, his choice could become more regret, if he was forced. In her mind, she knew she had to step back, walk away from him like she did with Grandmother Julia. It felt like she was giving up on him with every part of her heart. She forced herself to make these feelings strong, for him to lean on and not batter him with them anymore.

"I love you, Harry."

He refused to acknowledge her affections. Laura quietly left Harry where she had found him. In the few months of her death, she had gone through immense growth. She found more questions confronted her than answers. But the answers were there, she just had to discover them.

CHAPTER 20

Something had woken Sarah. She lay in bed and listened. The only thing she heard was the rain falling on the roof and tapping at the windows. Downstairs, the gentle tick-tock of the grandfather clock was interrupted as it chimed the half hour. Sarah rolled over to check the time. The glowing green numbers read 3:30am in the darkness. She shifted the blankets over herself and closed her eyes with a sigh.

After a few minutes Sam started snoring. There was nothing quiet about it. Sarah rolled over again, purposefully bumping into him as she felt for a comfortable spot. Sam quit snoring as he rolled onto his side. Sarah didn't bother to close her eyes as she fingered the eyelet lace edge of the sheet. She was wide awake now. The soft pitter-patter of rain could not lull her back to sleep.

The clock blinked away two more minutes. Sarah carefully slid out of the bed so not to wake Sam. She walked across the room and she gazed at their wedding picture during flashes of lightning while she fingered Laura's old silver plated mirror and brush sitting on the dresser. Sam mumbled in his sleep and she decided to go downstairs and make a cup of tea. She sat at the dining room table that was covered with stacks of black and white pictures and piles of file folders.

Sarah opened the black photo album and glanced at the pictures she had studied so intently over the past few months. It was full of fragile black and white photos with memories just as delicate. She loved the picture of Sam's great grandmother, Julia, and great grandfather, Levi. They sat so stiffly without even a hint of a smile, the trend for photographs at that time. It should have been a happy occasion as family lore had called it their wedding picture. Sarah picked up a pile of tin types and sorted through them. No one was sure who the people were, they had died, taking their memories with them. Aside from a few photographs or stories about these people they virtually disappeared without traces of their life. Now, her dear mother-in-law, Laura, could only be a memory.

Sarah furrowed her brow hoping that none of the memories she had of Laura would be forgotten. She went back to the album and stopped at the family picture of Laura and Peter with Sam and Karen as little kids, dressed in their Sunday best. Smiles adorned their faces with the painted on color to each person's lips and cheeks and eyes to make them twinkle. She adored this picture. There were tons of pictures scattered around the house of Sam and Sarah together. Each picture was a reminder of the happiness they had found in each other. The only thing absent from each photograph was children.

Her thoughts moved to the mother who abandoned her at the hospital. She wondered what it was like for that woman and if it was possible for her to have forgotten the infant she left so many years ago. Was that woman young or single or did she feel sorrow for not ever finding out what happened to the child Sarah had been. Had she been afraid? There were so many answers to questions that she would never know. How could that woman forget when Sarah thought of her constantly, but without any memories to hold on to?

Sarah wanted to believe she and Sam could have a baby who would ease her own pain over the elusive woman who gave birth to her. If she had a baby, it would be a connection, a true connection to another person in her life and world. Perhaps that woman had forgotten her, but Sarah's own baby would grow up knowing her.

Her mind was floating in a sea of unhappiness where Sam could not rescue her. Sarah could not keep her feelings locked in any longer. She wanted to yell at him for help, she wanted him to save her, but time was elapsing and the distance was growing between them. The thing she wanted the most and her greatest fear separated her from him. While he was sure she was part of his family, she felt like an outsider. Reaching out to him made her feel weak when he tried to reassure her with words that could not penetrate her convictions.

Gazing back over the pile of black and white photos, her eyes registered her own arm resting near them. Maybe the darkness of her own flesh was a symbol of how she was not destined to fit in with the people in the pictures. White people looking out of black pictures. Summer tans were as dark as those people became, such as the picture of men playing baseball in a field of grass with the trees acting as outfielders.

Sarah jumped at the flash of lightning and the sound of thunder following so close behind. She then felt a presence in the room with her. Without explanation she felt Laura's presence. Oddly, she felt no fear, but peace and serenity. Laura had been dead for months. Sarah wondered if Laura's spirit could have found its way back. If only she could have Laura's comforting ways to remind her that she did belong to a family and she would not be alone. Suddenly, she felt a feeling she had not experienced before in her misery. *'Don't forget me,'* a voice sounded in her head. It was someone else's fear Sarah was feeling. She could almost believe it was Laura calling out to her. *'Don't forget me. I haven't forgotten you.'* Sarah was quite sure she could feel Laura's pain left by the void of her own that had disappeared.

"Don't worry about me," Sarah whispered. "Sam and I will be okay." A tear ran down her cheek. "We're going to have a baby."

Sarah heard the words and wanted to question what she had just said out loud. There was no one there to hear her answer to a question she felt she had been asked. She had made a statement that would have been a lie or wishful thinking only moments ago. But in her heart, her entire body knew it was right. A baby. No longer would she be looking at the pictures of Sam's family like a stranger. She would now belong to all of them. She would even have connection to those in the unidentified pictures. Sarah imagined she could hear the whisper of Laura's voice say, *'you're family now,'* with a sound of a baby giggling in the background. She closed the photo album and got up to go back to bed. She and Sam would be okay. They would have a baby.

CHAPTER 21

The navy blue SUV slowed down as it came to the center of town. The local post office sat on the northwest corner, a mom and pop restaurant on the next, a red brick church with a white steeple across the street and an antique shop on the last corner. The shop was a little grey Victorian house with white gingerbread. Old chairs, a cast iron bath tub, an iron gate, a wooden butter churn and an assortment of other odds and ends cluttered the front porch and spilled onto the front lawn. Sam turned south as Sarah gazed out the window, watching the houses thin out quickly from the center of town.

To the east, the lake twinkled sun pennies as it began to peek through the trees that grew between the lake and the road. The snow that fell the night before was melting under the bright sun. They passed a park with empty picnic tables overlooking the beach. Past the park, tombstones appeared and Sam slowed down. They pulled into the second drive of the cemetery and parked near a majestic oak tree. Sarah got out of the passenger side and opened the back door.

"Wake up sleepy head," Sarah said to the little face in back.

"Do you want some water, Sarah?" Sam asked, opening the door on the back of the vehicle.

"Yeah, that would be good," she answered.

The little face broke out into yawns. Sarah unfastened the seat belt and set the little girl on the ground.

"Where's Grandma and Grandpa?" The little one asked, looking around.

"We're going to look for them," Sam said.

The little one started running between rows of headstones with the damp ground sucking at her pink rubber boots. Her three year old chubby legs, full of energy, kept going.

"Laura Julia," Sarah called after the little one. "We're going this way."

She ran back to her parents.

"I'm hot," Laura Julia said wiping sweat off of her forehead. "Can I have some water, Daddy?" Sam kneeled down and helped his daughter drink from the plastic bottle. After a few slurps Laura Julia ran ahead of her parents, looking back frequently to see if she was on the right course.

Half way down the row, Sam and Sarah stopped.

"Is this it? Is this it, Mama?" Laura Julia danced around a headstone.

"Yes, Laura Julia, it is." Sarah knelt down to trace a name with her finger. "See, there's Grandma's name, the same as yours."

"She gave me her name," Laura Julia said.

"Yes, baby. We gave you her name." Sam said.

Sarah gave the little girl a sheet of paper. "Here Laura Julia, put this over Grandma's name and you can color it with this crayon." Sarah tore the paper off of the crayon and rubbed it long ways across the paper. Laura Julia took the crayon from her and repeated what her mother had shown her.

"Gently, we only want a picture of it, we don't want to leave any crayon on her headstone."

"Look, Daddy," Laura Julia said. "There's numbers here."

"Those are the dates when Grandma was born and died."

"I need more paper," Laura Julia said, handing the colored one back. "I have to do Grandpa's now."

Laura Julia intently rubbed the crayon over the paper as letters and numbers almost magically appeared.

"Here's my Uncle Andrew and my Uncle Harry," Sam said, pointing at two simple headstones in the next row.

"Can I do them too, Daddy?"

"Sure, honey." Sarah handed Laura Julia more paper.

"My grandparents, Martha and James are over here," Sam pointed. "My great grandfather, Levi, is in the next row."

"It's still a mystery though," Sarah said. "No one knows what happened to Julia."

They looked at the headstones in silence until Laura Julia finished coloring.

"Can we go to the park?" Laura Julia asked.

"Just for a little bit," Sam said. "Then we have to go back to Aunt Karen's house for Easter dinner."

"Do you think Grandma and Grandpa will be at the park?" Laura Julia inquired.

"It doesn't matter where you are Laura Julia," Sarah kneeled down to Laura Julia and placed her little hand over her heart. "Grandma and Grandpa will always be with you in your heart."

At the park, Laura Julia stood at the lake's edge and found rocks to throw into the water, clapping her hands together after each one broke the surface with a plunk. Sam and Sarah sat next to each other on a nearby picnic table and watched. Through the trees, a few decorated with purple flower buds, separating the park from the cemetery, Laura was making her way towards her family to watch her grand-daughter. The wind swept across the water and blew a few strands of her graying hair around her face. She was older looking now and feeling older too. She had found peace but the journey was not over.

Death had given Laura a second chance to understand what life would not let her. She found that loving someone was not enough, forgiving was not enough either. It was agonizing to know she could not save Little Andrew or Harry or Grandmother Julia or even Sarah from their own regrets. Her convictions proved to be wrong when she attempted to take Harry's burden from him, endure the pain herself, as if it would be less heart wrenching if she could go through it instead. Nor could she ever be convincing enough to demolish the huge barricades Little Andrew surrounded himself with, built by his own fears, which kept him from moving on.

When she realized that she could not take Grandmother Julia's burden for her, it did not feel like love at first. Being supportive was not the hard work, but it was holding, biting her tongue and allowing Grandmother Julia to make mistakes, because she was not listening anyways, only resenting what she did hear. Mother had tried to teach her over and over, that the best lessons learned were from one's own mistakes and not because someone wanted you to learn it.

Laura struggled to separate which were her regrets and what were other family member's regrets and fears. When she didn't make them her own anymore, giving them back to the rightful owner, she was able to clearly work on her own fears. Only after determining what was truly hers and what belonged to others, was she able to remember the question Sarah had asked her. It had felt like watching the morning glories that grew up strings on the side of her mother's porch, the morning sun inviting the blossoms to open their faces.

Laura stood behind Sam and Sarah and watched them beam at Laura Julia playing in the water. She was sure Sarah's feelings of family connection were complete after years of no one else to call family. Sarah could now know how deep the connection was of shared blood with her beautiful daughter. Laura knew it would have been hard, if not impossible for Sarah to move on without Laura Julia. She now had a child she could call her own.

Laura felt privileged to give Sarah a gift where she would know her own flesh and blood. Hating another person for their skin color was wrong, but Laura had never before considered someone could hate them self for their skin color and found it vicious. That would be something Sarah would have to learn herself. It would be up to Sarah to stop hating the blackness of her skin, and not become like Grandmother Julia, who shackled herself with cravings and wants that never were, chaining her heart from resolving certain things that would never change. *"…even if it means leaving a part of me behind,"*

Through this child with Sarah's glowing tawny skin and soft dark eyes, framed in upside down smiles, which even Grandmother Julia would have adored, there was all kinds of hope. There was no doubt that Grandfather Levi would learn to love the rest of his family. Harry might move on, might forgive himself. Little Andrew would only follow in Harry's wake. Karen, for the rest of her life, would do right, as she saw was appropriate in her own logic, like her father Peter, letting his memory continue to live on.

Laura watched Sarah pulled Sam close to her.

She was close enough to hear Sarah say to Sam, "We're going to have another baby. Maybe it will be a boy this time."

Laura smiled broadly. She was going to be a grandmother again. *If I ever have a little girl, can I call her Laura?* The full memory of Sarah's visit to the nursing home was clear and Laura remembered the question Sarah had asked. She would not be forgotten. Turning, she started back towards the clearing and watched the snow hanging on the littlest stems in tufts of white, fall to the earth in heavy puffs. It would melt and flow toward the frozen creek with the weedy bottom, to the silty sand and then the cobbled bottom of the lake. More and more would follow the path, releasing frozen leaves, still-life's of the past season. With crescendos of illuminating warmth, the sun would disappear and rest behind the grey clouds that filled a memory of blue sky.

Inhaling the earthy smell of spring dampness, she breathed deeply, forcing herself to remember the freshness of the pine and the spice of autumn leaves, wanting to never forget what was comforting.

ACKNOWLEDGMENTS

Special thanks to Andrea Ferarra, editor extraordinaire, who read uncountable drafts of this story, listened to inordinate amounts of my whining and always rallied me by her belief in my writing skills.

Thanks to Dave Storer and LeAnn Keenan for their support and writing conferences.

Thank you is not enough for my husband who has encouraged me with every word I have written so far.

ABOUT THE AUTHOR

Emma Donaldson is an enthusiast for good food and the great outdoors. Within the boundaries of the state where she resides, she can find both and she believes it is hard not to be romantic and sentimental when one calls Michigan home.